FLYNN

A CHRISTIAN ROMANTIC SUSPENSE

OATH OF HONOR

LAURA SCOTT

Taylor Templeton frowned at the sound of breaking glass. It was three in the morning and she was giving three month old Max his bottle. She rose, cradling the baby close and moved toward the nursery door. A wave of apprehension made her turn and douse the small lamp on the nightstand, plunging the room into darkness.

The Millers were asleep, or so she assumed. Robin and Steve Miller were distant cousins on her mom's side of the family. When they'd learned she had experience as a live-in nanny, they'd hired her to help with Max now that Robin Miller had returned to work. The large two-story house in Brookland, Wisconsin, was very nice, and the Millers were decent people.

She hovered in the open doorway, listening intently. Had she imagined the sound? Maybe Robin or Steve had woken up in the middle of the night and had dropped a glass of water. She could be battling fear for no reason at all.

Then a creaking sound reached her ears.

Someone was coming up the stairs!

Without giving herself time to think, she darted across

the hall from the nursery to her bedroom. She left both doors open, fearing that closing them would catch the attention of whoever was coming up the stairs. Then she grabbed her phone from the nightstand where she'd had it charging.

The thud of a footstep on the landing made her shrink away from the bed. Spotting the walk-in closet, she quietly opened the door and stepped inside. She didn't close the door because it sometimes squeaked. Besides, she had to assume the intruder was looking for money, and if so, he would have no reason to come inside her room.

Or so she hoped.

Pressing herself in the corner of the closet against her clothes, she fought to breathe normally, despite the frantic beat of her heart. Her last live-in nanny assignment had brought a level of danger, so it was possible she was over-reacting.

Steve could have dropped the glass, then cleaned it up, and was returning to the master suite. Yes, the more she thought about it, the more she realized she was being ridiculous. There was no reason to be afraid.

She stepped toward the partially open closet door.

Pop! Pop! Pop! Pop!

The four shots were somewhat muffled but loud enough to reach her. Every muscle in her body froze at the implication.

Gunfire? Had the intruder shot and killed the Millers?

Taylor opened her mouth to scream but managed to swallow the sound without uttering a word. She needed to call 911, but her fingers didn't want to cooperate. Max continued to suckle his bottle, thankfully oblivious to the danger.

Then she saw a man dressed in black moving past the open doorway of her room. She caught a brief glimpse of his face, especially his prominent nose and bearded face. Her heart nearly burst out of her chest as she recoiled back from the closet door. She lowered herself to the floor, scooting into the corner and bending over to make herself as small as possible.

She didn't dare call 911, fearing the sound of her voice would lead the gunman to her hiding spot. Instead, she opened her text message app and scrolled through to the last message she had exchanged with Flynn Ryerson, a Milwaukee cop she'd met on her last assignment. She always kept her phone on silent, so she didn't hesitate to send a text, despite knowing he wouldn't likely see it at this hour of the morning.

A gunman is in the house!

She held the phone screen against Max's blanket to minimize the glow of light. The seconds ticked by with excruciating slowness. Then she saw the flash as Flynn responded.

Get out!

I can't. He's in the hallway. I'm hiding in the closet with the baby.

Where?

Taylor texted him the address. The minute she hit send, a muffled thud sent her pulse skyrocketing. Was the intruder looking for the baby?

For her?

Lord Jesus, keep us safe in Your care!

Knowing Flynn was on the way, Taylor tried to remain calm. Maybe the gunman wouldn't stick around. She belatedly realized Max had stopped taking the bottle. She needed to burp him but was afraid to move. He squirmed in her arms as if he were uncomfortable. What if he started to cry?

Bitter fear coated her tongue. With exaggerated slowness, she placed her phone screen down on the floor beside her to free up her hands. Gently shifting the baby in her arms, she settled him upright against her shoulder. She prayed he wouldn't start crying or make any other sound that would give them away.

He didn't.

Rubbing circles over Max's back, she strained to listen. The silence was not reassuring. She half expected the closet door to swing open revealing the gunman.

But then she heard more footsteps. Was the gunman leaving? She was afraid to move, to take another look.

Max burped. She held her breath, hoping and praying the gunman hadn't heard the sound. If he was really heading down the stairs, it wasn't likely.

A flash of light nearly made her scream. A flashlight? Was the intruder still searching for them? Biting her lip hard to keep from crying out, she sat frozen with Max on her shoulder, expecting the beam of light to grow closer.

Then it was gone.

She held her breath until she grew dizzy. By some miracle, Max had fallen asleep against her. She stayed where she was, imagining the intruder going methodically through each room in the house.

A wailing police siren filled her with hope. She felt certain that Flynn had called 911 on her behalf and that the local cops were well on their way. She forced herself to stand, using the wall for support as her knees felt like overcooked noodles.

Taylor peered through the gap of the half-open closet door. She didn't see anyone, and she couldn't hear anything either.

Except for the sirens that grew louder and louder.

If the intruder was smart, he'd bolt out of there before the cops arrived. Still, she hesitated, fear crippling her. Then she heard a loud crash of a door being forced open. She jumped, startling the baby.

"Taylor? Where are you?"

Flynn's shout was accompanied by the sound of pounding footsteps. She moved toward the doorway of her room, risking a quick glance out the door. She nearly sobbed in relief as Flynn rushed toward her.

"Taylor. Are you okay?" He wrapped his arms around her and Max. "You're not hurt?"

"F-fine." She was shivering, partially from the cold, but more so because of the horrifying experience. "Y-you need to ch-check on Robin and Steve. I—heard gunshots. Four gunshots."

Flynn's expression was grim as he turned to look over his shoulder. She noticed now that two uniformed officers had followed him up the stairs. They took a moment to poke their head into the nursery, then made their way down the hall, their weapons raised as they approached the closed door of the master suite.

Taylor turned her face into Flynn's shoulder as the officers opened the door and entered the room. It didn't take long for them to return.

"Two victims, male and female, were killed in their bed," an officer with the name tag of Rawson said grimly. "Each victim was shot twice."

"Robin and Steve Miller." She whispered the names of Max's parents. The news was exactly what she'd expected, but hearing the blunt words sent a wave of panic washing over her. Not just because the baby in her arms was now an orphan.

No, the worst part was that she'd gotten a glimpse of the gunman. She was the sole witness to a double homicide.

And from the way that guy had stealthily entered the home and ruthlessly killed Max's parents, she felt certain he wouldn't balk at finding and silencing her too.

FLYNN DID NOT like this situation one bit. He glanced at the Brookland PD officers who were regarding Taylor with veiled suspicion.

"This is Taylor Templeton. She's a live-in nanny," he explained. "I know her from a previous case."

The officers exchanged a dubious glance. "That's fine. We'll need her to come down to the station for questioning."

"I know, and she will. But she deserves a chance to change her clothes and get stuff for the baby." Flynn's blood ran cold at the thought of the gunman finding Taylor and the baby hiding in the closet. He wasn't even sure how he'd managed to wake up to her text message, but he was glad he had. He could feel her shaking and knew she was on the verge of a breakdown. Not that he blamed her. "Give us a few minutes, okay?"

"Fine. But don't touch anything outside these two rooms," Officer Rawson warned, gesturing to Taylor's room and the nursery.

When they were alone, he smoothed a hand down Taylor's back to reassure her. "I'm sorry about this, but you need to change and pack a bag. For yourself and the baby."

Taking a long, slow breath, she nodded and eased back. "Thank you for coming."

"Of course." He frowned. "Are you sure you're okay?"

"Um, yeah. I think so." She didn't sound at all confident. He eyed her with concern. Taylor was only twenty-four years old, much younger than his thirty-one, but appeared older now that she'd come face-to-face with death.

"Why don't you let me hold the baby?" He kept his tone soothing. "We can't stay here, Taylor. We need to go."

She seemed to pull herself together. "I know. Here, take him. His name is Max." She gently pressed the baby into his arms. "I don't understand why this is happening," she murmured as she turned to grab an overnight case from the closet. "Why would someone murder the Millers?"

"I don't know." Flynn gazed down at the sleeping baby lying in the crook of his elbow. The poor kid had barely come into this world and was already an orphan. Then he glanced back at her. "But rest assured the police won't stop until they find and arrest the man who did this."

She gave a jerky nod. "Will you please turn around so I can change? Don't leave," she quickly added, "just turn around."

Flynn did as she asked. He wanted to question her about what had transpired but reminded himself this wasn't his case. He was a Milwaukee tactical team police officer out of the seventh district. He and his teammates didn't have jurisdiction in Brookland.

However, the captain of their team, Rhyland Finnegan, happened to live in Brookland and knew many of the local police officers on a first-name basis. Rhy and their team lieutenant, Joe Kingsley—who happened to be married to Elly Finnegan, Rhy's baby sister—had a penchant for getting information from other jurisdictions.

It was a little early to call Joe or Rhy, so Flynn figured he'd wait until after Taylor had given her statement to contact his boss. Maybe by then he'd know more about what had transpired here.

His humble opinion was that this was a professional hit. Striking each victim with two gunshots was overkill, but it also sent a grim message.

And clearly Taylor was in danger now too.

"Okay. I'm ready."

He turned to find Taylor was dressed in a pair of snug blue jeans and a light-blue cable sweater. She had her blond hair pulled into a ponytail, her bright-blue eyes wide and fearful. She had a small suitcase on the floor beside her. He managed a smile. "You're all set?"

"I, uh, need toiletries from the bathroom." She swallowed hard, as if she were nervous about leaving the room. "Then I'll grab some things for Max."

"Let's go." He nudged the bedroom door open with his elbow. "You're safe now," he added.

"Am I?" She shook her head as she brushed past him. She darted in and out of the bathroom, shoving toiletries into her bag, then moved into the nursery. Five minutes later, she emerged with an overstuffed diaper bag.

Her suitcase and the diaper bag were stark reminders that traveling with a woman and a baby wasn't simple or quick. His buddy Zeke Hawthorne had experienced this firsthand a few weeks ago when he'd played the role of fiancé and bodyguard to his best friend's sister. Zeke had taken a bullet to the shoulder and was out on medical leave, or he'd have called him for backup.

Well, maybe not since Zeke and Sienna were engaged to be married for real and were also currently in Louisville for Sienna's next Christian music concert. No, he couldn't call Zeke, but there were seven other officers who would come to his aid if needed.

"We need to grab Max's car seat." Taylor's voice broke

into his thoughts as she headed down the stairs to the main floor. Still carrying Max, he followed.

"Ms. Templeton?" Another uniformed officer waited in the kitchen. "Are you ready to go with us to the Brookland PD?"

Flynn stepped forward. "I'll bring Ms. Templeton and the baby to you. That way I can take her someplace else when you're finished as she obviously can't stay here."

The officer frowned. "Who are you again?"

"MPD Officer Flynn Ryerson, I work for Rhy Finnegan's tactical team." Dropping his boss's name had the desired effect. The officer straightened and nodded.

"Oh yes, of course. We're familiar with Captain Finnegan. We'll meet you at the Brookland PD." The cop turned away, then paused to glance back at him. "You're not going to call Finnegan, are you?"

"Not at this time," Flynn said. "But depending on what happens next, I may have to." He gestured to the large home. "You do realize he's going to hear about this as we're only ten blocks from where he lives. This isn't the type of place where people are murdered in their beds."

The cop made a face. "Tell me about it."

Flynn noticed Taylor was shoving more items from the kitchen cupboard into the diaper bag. "Here, you take Max. I'll do that."

"No need. I have it." She used all her weight to press down on the stuff inside. Then she dropped her chin to her chest, heaving a sigh. "I don't know what to do."

He moved closer. "It's going to be okay. We'll get through this by taking one step at a time."

She lifted her head and quickly brushed tears from her eyes. She drew in a shaky breath. "Okay. I'm ready."

"Do you have a coat?" There had been frost warnings in

the news, which were not unusual for early November. "And where is the car seat?"

"My coat is in the mud room, and the infant seat is in the Millers' car." She gestured to the right. "They let me use their vehicle at times. Is it okay to go out there? I forgot I wasn't supposed to touch anything."

"You've been living here; your fingerprints are all over the place anyway." He understood Rawson's concern about preserving evidence, but if this was a professional hit, there wouldn't be much of anything to find. "Besides, there's no reason to believe he was in the mudroom or the garage. There's a broken window in the office that faces the back of the house. That appears to be the point of entry."

"Yes, I think so too. I heard the glass breaking." She shivered. "If I hadn't been awake and feeding Max . . ."

"Don't dwell on the what-if scenarios," he advised. "There's no point in looking backward. Let's just grab what we need to get out of here."

She gave a jerky nod and proceeded to the mudroom, which served as a first-floor laundry room as well. After donning a puffy navy-blue winter coat, she opened the garage door and flicked on the light.

He continued holding Max until she had the car seat out of the vehicle and sitting on the dryer. She rummaged in the diaper bag for a blanket, then took Max from his arms. With deft movements, Taylor buckled the sleeping baby into the car seat, then tucked the blanket around him for added warmth.

"I'll take that." He reached for the car seat. "My car is out front. Stay close to me, okay?"

"You don't think the killer is still out there, do you?" Taylor's blue eyes widened with apprehension.

"Not likely, but humor me." Flynn still experienced a

stab of guilt over the way he'd inadvertently put his team-mate in danger by trusting the wrong man. That had been almost a year ago, and he'd done his best not to let that slip paralyze him moving forward. Rhy had been unwaveringly supportive about the whole debacle. Still, Flynn tended to be more cautious these days.

He didn't want to make another mistake like that ever again.

Red and blue lights lit up the sky from the three responding squads parked in front of the house. Flynn fully expected more to arrive, along with the crime scene techs who would be tasked with collecting evidence from the house. The ME would be called in, too, even though there was no question about the cause of death. His black SUV was parked behind the squads, as he'd pulled up a minute after the officers.

And he had been extremely upset that they hadn't breached the house prior to his arrival. He'd taken the lead, kicking the front door in to gain access, even as the other officers had yelled for him to stay back.

Now those same officers gave him room to move past them mostly out of respect for Rhy Finnegan, not him specifically. He opened the rear passenger door and grimaced at the garbage that littered the back seat.

"Do you live your car or what?" Taylor asked, eyeing the mess.

"No. Sorry." His reputation of being a slob hadn't bothered him until now. With quick movements, he brushed the fast-food bags and crumpled napkins to the floor. Then he set Max's car seat down on the cushion.

"I'll do it." Taylor pushed him aside. "I suspect the front seat doesn't look much better."

Since she was right about that, he stepped back and

opened the front passenger door to clean off the seat for her. He took a moment to shove as much of the garbage into one of the larger fast-food bags to minimize the mess.

Still, there was no way to get rid of it all. Other than tossing what was left onto the floor of the front seat into the back.

Yeah, he really needed to do a better job of cleaning up after himself.

When that was finished, he took a moment to put Taylor's suitcase in the back before sliding in behind the wheel.

"Good grief," Taylor muttered as she settled into the newly cleared away passenger seat. She glanced at him with exasperation as she clicked her seatbelt into place. "I don't even want to imagine what your house looks like."

He shrugged as he started the engine. "It's not that bad."

"Yeah, why don't I believe that?" Her tone was lightly sarcastic, and he was glad she was thinking about something other than the brutal murders. Then as he pulled away from the curb, she asked, "How long will this take?"

"I'm not sure." He glanced at her. "I guess that depends on what you know about what happened."

She frowned. "I have no idea why someone broke into the house to murder the Millers. They're decent people from what I know. I've only been here for two weeks, but they've been nice enough. Not as demanding as some new parents I've worked with."

"You texted me that you were hiding in the closet," he said. "Was that after you heard the gunfire?"

"I'm not sure. Wait, yes, I think so." She shivered. "It all happened so fast. I heard the glass break first. Then the creak of the stairs. I left the nursery with Max to go into my room so I could grab my phone."

"Go on," he said when she paused.

"I hid in the closet, then thought I was being overly paranoid. I thought maybe Steve had accidentally dropped a glass of water and was returning to his room. I was about to step out of the closet when I heard the four gunshots." She drew in a ragged breath. "I froze, and that's when I saw him. The gunman walked right past my room."

"Wait, you saw him?" Flynn gaped at her. "You saw his face?"

"From the side, yes. He had a big nose and a beard." She scrubbed her hands over her face. "I shrank back into the closet and texted you. I was afraid he'd hear me or the operator if I called 911."

He nodded absently, still reeling from the fact that she saw the perp's face. Or rather the side of his face. Then a horrible thought struck. "Did he see you?"

"I don't think so." She frowned. "He looked around using a flashlight, but then left. I don't think he'd have walked away if he'd caught a glimpse of me hiding in the closet."

"No, probably not." Still, Flynn didn't like it. If the perp had swept his flashlight over the room, he had to have noticed the empty but obviously slept-in bed. He'd have to assume someone had been staying there.

"I heard the police sirens shortly after that," Taylor said. "I figured the sound scared him away."

"I'm sure it did." The news was hardly reassuring. The gunman had killed two people in their beds. Was it possible the perp had the means to learn that the Millers had hired a live-in nanny?

If so, Taylor Templeton could very well be next on the killer's hit list.

CHAPTER TWO

Taylor's stomach twisted painfully as she followed Flynn into the police station. He had insisted on carrying Max's car seat, while she had the diaper bag slung over her shoulder. Thankfully, the little boy was still sleeping.

She was concerned about the fate of the baby who'd lost his parents in a brutal murder. The reality of the situation still hadn't quite sunk in. Not only was Max an orphan, but she was in danger.

Not to mention needing a new job. And a place to live.

Maybe she needed to give up the idea of being a nanny and go back to working for a day care center. Two cases going bad in two months was too many.

"Please have a seat." An Officer Jones had escorted them back to an interview room. "Would you like coffee? Detective Klem will be here soon."

"Coffee would be great," she said, even though she wasn't the least bit tired.

"For me too," Flynn added as he set Max's car seat on the table. "Thanks."

Taylor dropped the diaper bag onto the floor and sank

into the closest chair. "Will they call the Department of Child Protective Services for Max?"

"Yes." Flynn's green eyes held hers. "I know how hard this is for you, but I'll stay close, okay?"

She tried to smile. "I know you take your duty seriously."

"It's not just duty," Flynn said, his gaze serious. "You witnessed a horrific crime. It's my job to keep you safe."

She appreciated Flynn's protection more than he knew. Four weeks ago when she'd first met Flynn, their personalities had clashed. She'd sensed how he'd looked down on her for being a live-in nanny. As if it wasn't a real job because all she did was take care of kids, most recently babies.

Flynn didn't realize the pay was decent, and the work was such that she often had downtime, which she had used to pursue her dream of writing a romance novel. Not that it was any of his business what she did for work.

After this most recent incident, she'd wondered if she'd taken the wrong path. Never before had she been in harm's way.

Until now.

"Here you go." Officer Jones returned carrying two cups of coffee. "Don't worry, this is from a fresh pot, not our usual sludge," he said jokingly to Flynn.

"Great." Flynn sipped from the cup.

She wrapped her hands around the cardboard cup, soaking in the warmth.

"It's going to be okay," Flynn said, breaking the silence.

Would it? She tried to nod, but just then the door opened, and a heavyset man came in. "Are you Taylor Templeton?"

"Yes." She straightened in her chair.

"I'm Detective Klem." He shook her hand, then turned

to do the same with Flynn. "I understand you were the live-in nanny for the Millers."

"Yes. But I only started two weeks ago." She glanced at Max who continued to sleep peacefully. "My job is obviously to care for the baby. I was feeding him when," she faltered, then added, "it happened."

Detective Klem nodded. "Would you mind starting from the beginning? Oh, and you need to know this interview will be recorded."

She glanced up at the camera mounted in the corner of the room, remembering every crime show she'd ever watched on television. Of course, she'd be recorded. She sighed and gathered her thoughts. "Max woke up crying. I went down to the kitchen to make him a bottle."

"Did you see anyone in the house? Or hanging around outside?"

"No." She shivered, wondering if the killer had been out there watching her. Then she decided he couldn't have been, or he'd have made sure to kill her too. "I was sitting in the rocker in the nursery feeding the baby when I heard glass breaking. I stood and moved to the doorway. When one of the stairs creaked, I dashed across the hall to my room to grab my phone."

Detective Klem nodded thoughtfully. "Then what happened?"

She stared down at her coffee. "I started to hide in the closet, then thought maybe Steve Miller had broken a glass and was headed to his room. I was about to step out of the closet with Max when I heard the four gunshots."

"You heard four gunshots?" Klem repeated.

"Yes. But with a brief pause between the first two and second two." She shivered, remembering. "I froze in the doorway. I was still holding Max when I saw the gunman pass by my bedroom."

The detective's bushy eyebrows shot up. "You saw him?"

She nodded. "But only from the side. White male, tall, with a large nose and bearded chin. He was dressed in black." Another detail popped into her head. "He wore thin black gloves. I . . . didn't see the gun, though. He must have had it in his right hand."

"Do you think you'd recognize him if you saw him again?" Klem asked.

"I honestly don't know. Maybe if I saw his profile I would, but it was dark, and I was scared out of my mind." She took a sip of her coffee.

"How old was he?" Klem asked.

She blew out a breath. "I would say twenties or thirties. His beard and hair were dark. No sign of gray. But I didn't see his full face, so it's hard to know for sure."

"I understand, and I'd like you to take a look at some mug shots," Klem said. "But first tell me what else you remember."

"I sat in the corner of the closet with Max and texted Flynn. I—we met before, and I was too afraid to call 911 in case he heard me talking. It was shortly after that when I saw the beam of his flashlight playing around the room."

"He had a flashlight and a gun?" Klem asked.

"I think so." She wished she'd paid more attention. "I didn't see either of them in his hand, just the left hand covered in a black glove. But I know there was a beam of light that shone into the room. I was scared he'd find us in the closet, but he didn't. I assume the sound of police sirens scared him off."

Despite the recording, she noticed the detective took

notes on a pad of paper before looking up at her again. "Then what happened?"

She glanced at Flynn. "Flynn and the other officers arrived."

Detective Klem sat back in his chair. "What do you know about the Millers?"

"I—not a lot. They're second cousins on my mom's side of the family, but I never met or interacted with them before they hired me to be their nanny."

"What do they do for work?" Klem asked.

"Steve Miller is the president of Brookland Bank, and Robin does some interior designing." She managed a wry smile. "Apparently, Robin's most recent client was one of the big-name players from the Milwaukee Bucks. She was excited, hoping that word would spread to other famous athletes." Her smile faded as she realized Robin Miller would not design anything ever again.

"Bank and interior design," Klem repeated thoughtfully. "Interesting."

"You're thinking the banker was the most likely target for the professional hit," Flynn said, speaking up for the first time.

Klem shrugged, then slowly nodded. "Gotta follow the money. And as you say, this whole situation reeks of cold professionalism. Not a crime of passion."

"I didn't notice that anything in the house was taken," Flynn went on. "From what Taylor is describing, it doesn't sound like the perp had much time to search the place."

"We have the crime scene techs out there now, but you're right," Klem admitted. "From what I've been told, the place looks remarkably undisturbed."

Taylor shivered. "Robin has a cleaning service too.

They come in weekly on Tuesdays." She had to think for a moment. "Today is Thursday, right?"

"Yes, that's good information. If we do find any fingerprints not belonging to you or the family, that may help," Klem said. "We'll need your prints so we can rule yours out. And I'd like your phone number too."

"Okay." Being fingerprinted and providing her contact info was the least she could do to help find the man who'd killed Steve and Robin Miller. "I'm happy to look at mug shots, although I'm not sure I'll be able to recognize the gunman. But what about the baby? Max Miller?" She rested her hand on the infant car seat. "What's going to happen to him?"

"We'll keep him here until someone from the Department of Health and Human Services can get here to take him." Detective Klem reached over to pat her hand. "Don't worry, I'm sure he'll go into a good home."

She wanted to believe that, but it wasn't easy. She'd gotten attached to the little boy. "I can watch him here until they arrive," she offered.

"That would be great," Klem said. "Anything else you can tell us about the Millers? Has anyone been to visit them lately?"

"Not that I'm aware of." She thought about Steve's home office. Flynn had mentioned that was the point of entry. "Steve sometimes works from home, but I haven't seen him meeting with anyone. I take Max out for long walks in the stroller, though, so it's possible someone had come in to visit while I was gone."

Detective Klem made another note on his pad. Then he glanced at Flynn. "Anything you care to add?"

Flynn pursed his lips. "Not much. I noticed the place was unusually clean, too, but that makes sense now that we know about the cleaning service. After Taylor texted me, I called 911, then rushed over to the house."

Klem lumbered to his feet. "Okay, sit here for a minute. We'll get your fingerprints and contact information on record first, then I'll bring in a laptop so you can look at mug shots. I'll run a search for guys with beards." He shrugged. "It might help narrow the field."

She nodded, then jumped to her feet when Max began to squirm. She caught the pungent scent and knew the baby was in dire need of a diaper change. "It's okay, big guy, I'm here." She lifted him from the car seat, holding him close as she reached for the diaper bag.

"Need help?" Flynn asked.

"No thanks." She glanced at him in surprise that he'd even offered. "I can change him."

Flynn moved her coffee cup and his out of the way. She pulled the changing pad from the bag and set Max on it. She cooed at the baby as she made quick work of unsnapping his onesie.

It bothered her to think of handing the baby over to strangers. Robin would be horrified.

There was no way she'd be allowed to step in as the baby's temporary guardian. But maybe someone on her mom's side of the family would offer to do so. That possibility cheered her up, and she made a mental note to call her aunt Jeannie later. Jeannie was another one of her mother's sisters.

Her parents were out of the country on a month-long trip to Europe. She didn't want to bother them about this now.

By the time she'd finished with Max, Detective Klem returned with the computer. After taking her fingerprints, he set up the computer. She held the baby in her lap as she worked the mouse to begin going through the mug shots. Focusing on the profiles of each criminal, she tried to mesh the face on the screen with the flash of memory she had in her mind.

But after a solid hour of searching, she wanted to scream. Either the guy wasn't in the system or she hadn't gotten a good look at him.

And she feared the latter.

Flynn had taken over carrying Max, pacing from one side of the conference room to the other as she'd worked. With a frustrated gesture, she pushed the computer aside and stood. "I don't see him, and I can't sit here anymore. Will you please take me home?" As soon as the word left her mouth, she realized she didn't have a home.

There had been no reason to pay for an apartment in her current role. And she didn't want to go back to living with her parents. Sometimes when she was between jobs, she'd stayed in a rental.

Yet the idea of being all alone wasn't appealing.

As if reading her mind, Flynn handed the baby to her. "I'll take you to my place," he said. "I have a guest room, so you'll have the privacy you need."

She was grateful for the offer but pretended to think about it. "I don't know. Based on what I saw in your car, I can't help but wonder what I'm walking into. Are you going to expect me to clean the house?"

He laughed, and for the first time since this nightmare started, a genuine smile tugged at her mouth. "I can't lie; it's probably messy, especially compared to what you're used to. But no, I don't expect you to clean. I can manage that. This is a no-strings offer."

"Okay, thanks." Staying with Flynn wasn't a long-term plan, but she needed to figure out her next steps. She swayed back and forth with Max, glancing at her watch. The hour was still relatively early, seven in the morning, and she had no idea what time the representative from child protective services would show up. "You better let Detective Klem know I couldn't find the gunman."

Flynn nodded and opened the door to the interview room. Then he stepped back as Detective Klem and another woman happened to be standing there. At first, Taylor thought the woman was from CPS, but then she saw the gun on her belt.

She inwardly groaned, not in the mood to start all over with another interview. She was tired, hungry, and on edge.

"I'm Detective Irving," the woman said in a brisk no-nonsense tone. "I was hoping you'd answer a few more questions."

"New questions?" Flynn asked, stepping next to her as if she needed his protection. "Or going through the information she's already given Detective Klem?"

Irving's face flushed red, then she tipped her chin defiantly. "I want to hear what our witness has to say for myself."

"Nope, not happening," Flynn said. "You can watch the recording. We're leaving."

"What about the baby?" Klem nodded at Max. "I thought you agreed to stay and watch him until the CPS worker gets here?"

Taylor looked down at the baby in her arms, then at Flynn. With a resigned nod, she sank back into her seat.

She had promised to watch over Max. Answering more questions while she waited seemed like the least she could do.

FLYNN REMEMBERED Jina's less than favorable interaction with Detective Irving, and after listening to her question Taylor, he was not impressed. The female detective came across as antagonistic and sarcastic. As if Taylor was the criminal and not the witness.

They were interrupted by a knock at the door. Seeing a woman hovering next to a uniformed officer, he knew the caseworker from CPS had finally arrived.

He stood. "This interview is over."

Irving sputtered with anger, but Klem looked relieved as he shot to his feet. "I understand. Come on, Irving. There's nothing new to be learned here. Let's give Ms. Templeton room to discuss the baby's care with the Department of Child Protective Services."

Flynn thought Irving would resist leaving, but just then Max began to cry. As if sensing there was no point in pushing for more, Irving followed Klem out of the interview room.

He stayed out of the way as Taylor went through Max's routine. "He's probably hungry again," she said as his wailing increased. "I can make another bottle for him before you go."

"I'll do it." Flynn held out his hand. "It can't be that hard."

Taylor flashed a relieved smile and dug the bottle and formula supplies from the bag. "Two scoops and fill it all the way with warm—but not hot—water, okay?"

"Got it." He took the items from the room, stopping abruptly as he saw Klem and Irving arguing.

"You should have called me," Irving said.

"I did," Klem shot back. "Don't blame me because you didn't hear your phone."

Flynn felt sorry for Klem. It couldn't be easy to be partnered with Irving. In the small kitchenette, he filled the baby bottle with warm water, added the formula, and shook it vigorously to dissolve the powder. As he was leaving, he heard a voice call out, "Klem! Call for you on line two!"

He wasn't a detective, and this wasn't his case, but Flynn hovered in the doorway of the breakroom, trying to listen in on Klem's side of the call.

"Yeah, that's good that a print was found in the office. Let me know if you get a hit in the system. We're heading over to the bank to start interviewing employees now," Klem said. "Appreciate the update."

Flynn walked out of the kitchenette, giving Klem a nod. "You're following up on the bank angle?"

Klem frowned, but then nodded. "Yeah. As you said, I doubt anyone doing interior design would be the target of a professional hit. I'll be in touch with Ms. Templeton if we find someone matching the description of the shooter."

"Sure." He wondered about the fingerprint that was found in Steve Miller's office, but there was no point in asking as it hadn't been run through the system yet. Still, he intended to let Rhy know about this, so his boss could follow up with the case.

Taylor's eyes were bright with tears as she handed Max over to the CPS caseworker. "Please take good care of him," she said.

"We will," the woman assured her. "And thanks for the information on the possible family connections. Placing children with relatives is always preferable in these situations."

Taylor nodded and wiped her eyes. "I'll call my mom too. She and my dad are on a month-long cruise, but I'd like to let her know what happened."

That made him frown, and as he escorted Taylor

through the Brookland PD, he spoke in a low voice. "I'm not sure you should reach out to your parents yet."

"Why not?" She sounded crabby, and he couldn't blame her.

"We don't know who this guy is or what he's capable of." He opened the passenger door of his SUV for her. "Let's give Brookland PD some time to investigate first, okay?"

She waited until he was in the driver's seat and backing out of the parking space, before saying, "You really think he's going to come after me?"

"I don't know." He wished he could reassure her, but he hadn't liked hearing how the gunman had played his flashlight over her room. If Taylor hadn't texted him when she had, and the Brookland PD hadn't responded so quickly, he was very much afraid that Taylor and Max would have been ruthlessly shot and killed. "But I'd rather not take the risk."

"I don't believe this," she whispered. "I thought what happened to Sienna was bad, but this is much worse."

"Yeah. But you're safe with me." He tried to smile. "And the good news is that the one meal I can cook is breakfast. I have bacon, eggs, and toast at home if you're hungry."

"I am hungry, although it seems wrong." She pulled the ponytail holder from her blond hair and combed her tresses with her fingers. "I just can't believe they're gone. That they were involved in anything that would cause someone to shoot them while they were sleeping."

"Detective Klem is a good guy; he'll figure out what happened."

"I know." She glanced at him. "I really appreciate your help, Flynn. I feel bad I dragged you into this, but contacting you was the only option that flashed in my mind."

"Hey, I don't mind," he said lightly. "Good thing I live in Greenland. I was glad to have gotten there so fast."

"You have a house?" she asked.

"Yes, it's small, only two bedrooms." It was more than enough to suit his needs. Yet he also knew it would be a drastic change from the sprawling dwelling she'd lived in with the Millers. "Like I said, you can sleep in the guest room."

"I'm not sure I'll be able to sleep without nightmares," she confessed.

He didn't have a good response for that. In his role as a police officer, he'd seen more than his share of violence. But that was his job, to protect and serve. Being a live-in nanny shouldn't be dangerous.

And for sure a nanny shouldn't be the witness of a double homicide.

A glance in the rearview mirror made him frown. Dawn was barely peeking over the horizon now that they'd fallen back from daylight saving time, but the vehicle behind him had two headlights, one slightly brighter than the other.

The same set of headlights had been behind him on the way to the police department from the Millers' home in Brookland.

Were the cops following him for some reason? That didn't make any sense, but he couldn't seem to shake off the weird coincidence.

Without warning Taylor, he abruptly turned at the next light, then hit the gas, surging forward. She cried out in alarm, bracing herself with a hand on the dash.

"What are you doing?"

"Sorry about that but hang on." The vehicle with the unevenly bright headlights had made the same turn.

"Are we being followed?" Taylor's tone was incredulous. She twisted in her seat to look behind them.

The sharp crack of gunfire had him yanking her down even as he swerved to get out of the line of fire. He cranked the wheel to cut through a gas station that was thankfully mostly empty. He hit the gas again, pulling into traffic and cutting off another driver. Ignoring the sharp blare of the guy's horn, he drove as fast as he could, going around cars that were moving too slow.

The morning rush hour made it that much more difficult to avoid the car tailing them. Although he hoped the same would hold true for the driver of the car with uneven headlights.

Using his thumb, he activated his phone. "Call 911!"

The sound of a ringing phone filled the interior of his car. A moment later, the dispatcher answered, "This is the 911 operator, what is your emergency?"

"This is MPD Officer Flynn Ryerson. Shots fired on Blakemore Drive," he said as he hit the brake to avoid striking another vehicle. He quickly swerved around the slow driver and then took another right-hand turn. "I'm heading west now, on 121st Street. Get officers to this area now!"

"Please stay on the line," the operator said calmly.

He thought he saw the uneven headlights closing the gap, so he quickly switched lanes and floored the gas, shooting through a yellow traffic signal. More horns blared, but then other cars moved into the intersection blocking the driver of the uneven headlights from following.

Flynn wasn't listening as the 911 dispatcher continued to talk. He was too busy trying to figure out where he could take Taylor that would be safe.

Not his place and not the American Lodge in Brookland either. He wanted to be as far away from Brookland and the scene of the murders as possible.

He thought of Zeke's house and made another abrupt turn. He felt certain his buddy wouldn't mind his using the place while he was out of town.

Especially not once Zeke heard that he needed to keep Taylor safe from the gunman hot on their tail.

CHAPTER THREE

The gunman had found them! Taylor had her head down as Flynn made frequent and unexpected turns. The seatbelt tightened painfully against her chest. She wanted to cry or scream, but she was frozen in place, much like when she'd heard the four gunshots that had ended Steve's and Robin's lives.

The only good news was that Max wasn't with them. The very thought of the baby sitting in the back seat as someone fired shots at them made her blood run cold. As hard as it had been to hand him off to child protective services, that was better than having him in danger.

She tried to swallow past the lump of fear in her throat. Gingerly lifting her head a few inches, she tried to see Flynn's face. He seemed to be driving normally now, or maybe she was just getting used to the jarring motions. "I-is he gone?"

"Yeah, I think I lost him." He glanced at her, then added, "But stay down anyway just in case."

In case the gunman returned. Flynn didn't have to say

the words that echoed in her mind. She couldn't fault him for being careful, so she lowered her head back down.

And silently thanked God for keeping them safe.

"Officer Ryerson? Are you there?"

Taylor had forgotten about the 911 dispatcher on the line.

Instead of answering, Flynn disconnected from the call. She lifted her head again. "Why did you do that?"

"There's no point in broadcasting our location." Flynn slowed the car, then surprised her by pulling into a driveway. "I'll make some calls once we're settled inside."

"Is this your home?" She eyed the small white house curiously.

"No, it belongs to Zeke who, as you probably already know, is out of town at the moment with Sienna." Flynn moved the gearshift into park. "Wait here. I need to open the garage door."

She nodded, watching as Flynn opened the flap of a keypad and entered a code. The large garage door rumbled upward, revealing an empty garage. She'd met Zeke and Flynn a month ago when a stalker had targeted Sienna who had hired Taylor to be a live-in nanny for her daughter, Bailey. Zeke and Flynn were obviously good friends, so she had no doubt that Zeke wouldn't mind them staying there for a few days.

Once Flynn had driven into the garage, he closed the garage door to hide them from prying eyes. He took a moment to grab her suitcase from the back seat, then led the way inside.

"I think you should take the main bedroom with the attached bath," Flynn said, carrying her bag through the house. She followed him down the hall to the large bedroom. "Sienna would like that."

She nodded, although it felt strange to be there.

Flynn turned to head back to the kitchen. "I hope they have something we can make for breakfast."

Her previous hunger had vanished during the crazy drive away from the gunman. But now that they were safe in a location that couldn't be connected to her, or Flynn for that matter, she knew she wouldn't make it all day without something to eat.

"I'll make coffee." She opened the cupboard doors to find what she needed, anxious for something productive to do.

"Coffee is here in the freezer," Flynn said, setting the bag of expensive dark coffee grounds next to the pot. "Looks like they have eggs and bacon, but no bread."

"That's fine." She was grateful for whatever was available. "We need to make sure to pay them for the groceries we use."

"I'll leave some cash behind," Flynn said. "But you know Zeke and Sienna probably won't take anything. They're too nice to worry about us eating some of their food."

He was probably right; Sienna was generous and sweet. She didn't know Zeke as well because Flynn was the one who'd stayed back to act as a bodyguard to her and Bailey.

A role she'd dragged him right back into just weeks later.

She moved out of the way as Flynn began to prepare breakfast. But then his phone rang.

"My boss," he said, glancing down at the screen. "I really need to fill him in on what's happened."

"Go ahead." She shooed him out of the way. She was perfectly capable of cooking breakfast. She'd done that and more household chores as part of her nanny duties.

Some parents took advantage, but others were simply thankful.

"Hey, Rhy," she heard Flynn say. "I've landed in the middle of an interesting situation involving a double homicide in Brookland."

There was a pause as Flynn listened. She started the bacon in one frying pan, then pulled out another for the eggs. Then she filled two mugs with coffee, setting one on the kitchen table for Flynn.

He thanked her with a warm smile. "You remember Taylor Templeton; she was the live-in nanny working for Sienna last month. Her newest job was being a nanny for Steve and Robin Miller, and they were murdered in their beds in what looks to me like a professional hit. Taylor saw the gunman while she was hiding in the closet with their three-month-old son."

She cracked the eggs into a pan, deciding to make them over easy as there wasn't any milk in the fridge for scrambled. Flynn continued to outline everything that had transpired at the Miller residence, all the way up to and including the way she'd gone through mug shots at the Brookland PD.

"After we left the precinct, I saw a car with uneven headlights following us," he continued. "I had noticed it earlier and managed to take a series of abrupt turns just as the driver took several shots at us. I called 911 and managed to lose the guy."

Another brief silence as Flynn sipped coffee while listening to what Rhy was saying.

"Yes, sir. I brought Taylor to Zeke's place since he and Sienna are out of town. I know Zeke won't mind, and it was easier and quicker to come here than to find a hotel. You know how it is, we're not exactly welcome at the City

Central anymore after damaging the suite last month, and I figured we should avoid the American Lodge because it's located in Brookland."

Taylor shivered, thinking about the near miss at the City Central Hotel. Flynn had suffered a flesh wound from a bullet that nicked his arm. He and Zeke had managed to get her, Bailey, and Sienna out safely.

That was the reason she'd reached out to him in the middle of the night. She and Flynn were complete opposites, but she'd known he'd protect her without hesitation.

"I would like to be kept in the loop on the double homicide investigation," Flynn said. "I heard something about a fingerprint being found in the homeowner's office. Steve Miller is the president of Brookland Bank; it stands to reason he was the primary target. His wife, Robin, does interior design for people with money for that kind of thing."

She took the strips of bacon from the pan, adding three slices for each of them to the plates, then she finished flipping the eggs and slid them onto the plates. She caught his eye as she held up the two plates, indicating breakfast was ready.

"Anything you can find out would be helpful," Flynn said, nodding at her. He crossed to the table. "I'm afraid I'll need to take some vacation time until the gunman has been found and arrested."

After setting the plates on the table, she turned to grab silverware and her coffee cup.

"Thanks, Rhy. I appreciate your help on this. I'll call for reinforcements as needed." He nodded at something, then said, "Yes, later." Ending the call, he set his phone aside. "We're set. Rhy told me to take as much time off as I need."

"Your boss sounds like a nice guy." She dropped into the

closest chair. "I seem to remember Zeke reaching out to him for help, too, when Sienna was in danger."

"We hit the jackpot with Rhy and Joe leading our tactical team," Flynn said. He sat beside her, then reached for her hand. "I'll say grace, the way Zeke and Sienna would if they were here."

"Okay." She bowed her head, keenly aware of the warmth of Flynn's fingers around hers. She'd attended church while growing up but hadn't lived it the way Sienna had. After spending time with Sienna and Bailey, Taylor had found herself leaning more and more on prayer.

"Lord Jesus, we thank You for this food we're about to eat. We ask You to continue to keep Taylor and Max safe in Your loving arms. Amen."

"Especially Max, as he deserves a family who will love him. Amen," she added.

"I know you're concerned about the baby, but I'm sure he'll be well cared for." Flynn took a bite of bacon. "This is great, thanks."

Thinking of Max made her sad, but she forced herself to eat, knowing she needed to be strong to get through this. "I hope you're right about Max being placed with a nice family. To be honest, I'm glad Max wasn't in the car earlier. I really don't understand how the gunman found us."

Flynn scowled. "He must have been hiding near the scene of the crime and watching the place when I drove up to the house. Either that or he was waiting near the police station, knowing you'd have to give a statement."

She stared at him. "But he didn't see me. I was hiding the entire time. I only happened to catch a glimpse of him walking past, but he didn't turn his head to look at me. If he had"—she stopped, swallowed hard—"he'd have shot me."

"I know that he didn't see you in time to get rid of you,"

Flynn agreed. "But the fact that he used a flashlight to look inside your bedroom indicates he knew there was at least one more person living in the home."

A cold chill washed over her. Because Flynn was right. The flashlight beam proved the killer had come back to try to find her but ran out of time after hearing the sirens.

It hadn't occurred to her until this moment that the gunman might know what she looked like.

And that he was likely more determined than ever to silence her once and for all.

FLYNN WISHED he could say something to reassure Taylor he wouldn't let this guy touch her, but they'd already been followed. And had been shot at.

He hated the thought of failing in his mission to keep Taylor safe. He should have anticipated the guy might stake out the Brookland police station.

He made a silent promise not to underestimate this guy again.

"Well, I guess that means I should keep going through mug shots," she said, after a prolonged silence. "It would be helpful for me to identify him before he finds me."

"Going through mug shots would help." He knew it would be better for her to do something constructive, even though he wasn't convinced the killer was in the system. "I'll ask Cassidy to bring a computer for us to use."

"Okay. That would be great." He appreciated her attempt to stay positive. "Are you sure Zeke or Sienna don't have a computer here we can borrow?"

He finished his breakfast, then rose to carry his plate to the sink. "I'll take a look around, but it might be better to have two computers anyway." He wasn't sure what he could do to help figure out who had a reason to kill Steve and Robin Miller, but he couldn't sit around doing nothing either.

Leaving the dishes in the sink, he refilled his coffee mug, then moved through the house. He didn't like invading Zeke and Sienna's privacy but reminded himself that his buddy wouldn't mind.

He found a laptop computer tucked away in a drawer. After setting it on the kitchen table, he plugged it in and turned it on. Of course, the device was password protected. Eyeing the clock on the microwave, he figured quarter to nine should be early enough for Zeke, Sienna, and Bailey to be up. Sienna might sleep in after a show, but a toddler would want to be fed.

Pulling out his phone, he texted Zeke a message asking for a call as soon as possible. Less than a minute later, his phone buzzed with an incoming call.

"Hey, Zeke, how are things in Louisville?" he asked.

"Actually, we're in Hot Springs, Arkansas, this week; Louisville was last week. Sienna is doing fabulous as always. Your text sounded urgent. What's going on?"

Flynn quickly filled Zeke in on Taylor's recent nanny position and everything that had transpired over the past few hours. "I hope you're not angry with me, but I brought Taylor to your house. It seemed best to avoid going to my place since the shooter followed us after leaving Brookland PD."

"Of course, I'm not mad, stay as long as you need. How horrible for Taylor to have witnessed a double homicide."

"Yeah. She narrowly escaped being shot and killed too." Hearing her name, Taylor shot him a quick glance from her position at the kitchen sink. "She wants to go through mug shots to see if she can ID the perp. I found your laptop but need the password."

"Of course." As Zeke rattled off the password, Flynn wrote it down on a sticky note, then typed it in using the keyboard. The screen sprang to life.

"I'm in, thanks." Flynn felt better knowing Zeke was on board with his bringing Taylor here. "I'll leave some cash for the food we're eating."

"No need, keep it as you're going to need it. I only care about you and Taylor staying safe," Zeke quickly reassured him. "You may need a replacement vehicle if you think the killer has your license plate number. If he's a professional hit man, he likely has connections and access to information."

"Yeah, I know. We're parked in your garage now, but I'll reach out to Cass soon." He trusted Cassidy's skills, and those of his other teammates, but he and Zeke had been close, and he missed having his friend covering his back. Not that Zeke could do much one handed. He'd been wounded back when the killer had almost kidnapped Sienna. "How's the shoulder?"

"Good according to the physical therapist." Zeke sighed. "But I feel like a weakling. I am only approved to lift a measly five-pound weight."

"Don't push it or you might damage the muscles and tendons worse than they already are," Flynn warned.

"Yeah, yeah," Zeke groused. "That's what Sienna says too. At least I'm able to do basic tasks with Bailey, or I'd really be a hindrance here."

Flynn realized that if Zeke hadn't been shot and wounded, Taylor might still be working for Sienna as Bailey's nanny rather than taking the position with the Millers.

It was strange the way things had worked out perfectly for Zeke and Sienna, but those same circumstances had thrown Taylor into the midst of danger.

He wasn't as familiar with the Bible as many of his teammates, but there was no doubt that God worked in mysterious ways.

"Do you need anything else?" Zeke asked.

"No, we're fine." He pulled himself back to the issue at hand. "Thanks again for being cool with us staying here. I'm sure Taylor will feel better about it now that you've given your stamp of approval."

"Anytime. Stay safe and let me know if you need anything else," Zeke said.

"Will do." Flynn ended the call, then thumbed through his contact list to find Cassidy's number. Thankfully, she answered right away too.

"Hey, Flynn. What's up?"

He sighed and went through the entire story for the third time in less than an hour. Cassidy had met Taylor before, so she was just as horrified over what had happened.

"I can't believe Taylor witnessed two brutal homicides," Cass said. "I can only imagine how scared she was hiding in the closet with a baby."

"She was very much so. And now we need your help," Flynn said. "Can you bring a computer and a replacement vehicle? We're staying at Zeke's home in Greenland."

"Of course, I can be there in an hour or so," Cassidy agreed. "Do you want a rental or to borrow my car?"

"A rental would be best. Can you get someone on the team to help?"

"Not a problem. Jina is back from her honeymoon. I'm sure she won't mind pitching in." Cassidy hesitated a moment, then said, "Flynn, how are you going to find a professional hit man?"

That was a really good question. One he wished he could answer. "So far our only option is to go through mug shots." He didn't like feeling helpless against an unknown foe. "I know Rhy will get any information he can out of the Brookland PD. Maybe they'll find a way to track the guy."

"I hope so." Cassidy didn't sound convinced.

He wasn't positive about that either, but he kept his tone light. "Call me when you're close."

"Will do. See you soon." With that, Cass ended the call.

He stared down at his phone for a moment, glad to know that Rhy and the rest of the team was unwavering in their support. Then he set the device aside to log into the police database. He knew how to perform a basic search, so he did so now, pulling up all males with black or brown beards in the age range of twenty to forty-five.

"Everyone knows all about this now, huh?"

Taylor's voice broke into his thoughts. He turned to catch her watching him. "Yes. But it's okay, as they're more than willing to help me keep you safe."

She nodded thoughtfully. "I appreciate that; it just seems so surreal. Like something out of a movie. Hearing you explain what happened is a stark reminder that I didn't dream it. That it really happened."

"Hey, it's okay." He rose and stepped forward, closing the gap between them. He took her hand. "You don't have to be afraid."

"I know." Her smile was lopsided. "Who would have thought that being a nanny would put me in danger?"

Flynn winced, knowing he'd made his feelings known when they'd first met. He honestly hadn't been impressed with Taylor's role as a live-in nanny. It seemed rather old-fashioned to him that a young woman would give up her independence to live with a strange family to care for their children.

A rich family, as most people couldn't afford to pay for that luxury.

But he had come to appreciate how much Taylor loved taking care of kids. Who was he to look down on her decision?

"I'm sorry if I made you feel as if your career wasn't worthwhile," he said. "That wasn't my intention. If I'm being honest, you're the first live-in nanny I've ever met."

She arched a brow. "I kind of figured that much. But thanks. I might not be as brave and dedicated as a cop, but kids hold the key to the future of our country."

"That's true," he said. "I hadn't thought of it like that."

She grimaced. "Yeah, well, this might be the end of my nanny career. It's probably safer to be a teacher or work at a day care center."

He wasn't sure what to say to that. It wasn't logical that those occupations she'd mentioned seemed more noble than being a nanny. He told himself he was letting his own past color his opinion. Just because his mother had scraped by as a waitress to provide for him and his younger sister, Fiona, didn't mean Taylor shouldn't make a decent living being a nanny to rich people's kids.

"I think you should do what makes you happy," he finally said. "Your opinion is the only one that matters."

She shrugged without saying anything more. He released her hand and gestured to the computer. "When you're ready to look at mug shots again let me know."

"I'm almost finished here." She turned back to the sink. "I'll rinse these and let them air dry."

"I can dry them," he said. "Just because I don't clean as often as I should doesn't mean I don't know how."

She shook her head ruefully. "I can't imagine driving around in a messy car."

It didn't bother him, but he didn't voice the thought. His teammates teased him mercilessly about being a slob, and he hadn't really cared.

Until now.

"I'll do better." He gently nudged her from the sink. "Go check the computer. I set up the search parameters for you to continue looking through mug shots."

She turned and dropped into the closest chair at the kitchen table. "Is there a way to narrow down the search to those mug shots I haven't already seen?"

"Yes, we did the search by name, and you had already made it through the first six letters of the alphabet. You can start with the letter *G*."

"I see that now, thanks." As she worked, he finished rinsing the dishes in the sink, then began toweling them dry.

He watched her, thinking not for the first time how beautiful she was. Too young and pretty for him, but that didn't mean he wasn't interested.

Flynn was not the chick magnet some of his teammates were. Quite the opposite. Most of the time women barely gave him a second glance. Growing up, he'd thought it was because they were poor or because he was cursed with red hair thanks to his Irish roots.

But now that he was older, he understood his features were plain, his red hair making him look younger than he really was. And he wasn't considered handsome in the classical sense.

It shouldn't matter, as he and Taylor were complete opposites. And she'd only texted him because he was a cop, and she happened to have his personal cell number from their interaction last month.

He shook off the thought, knowing he was letting the fact that everyone on their team was settling down, getting married, and having kids get to him. Even Jina, who was their team's sharpshooter, had found the perfect guy for her. And he'd have bet his paycheck Jina would never settle down.

Cassidy was still single, but it was no secret their team tech expert, Gabe Melrose, had a crush on her. The only one who was oblivious to that was Cass herself.

When the dishes were put away, he picked up his phone. He wanted to text Rhy to see if he was able to get any information out of the Brookland PD but reminded himself it had only been an hour since he'd spoken with his boss.

An hour that seemed like ten, he thought with a heavy sigh.

He dropped into the seat beside Taylor, eyeing the screen as she went slowly and methodically through the mug shots. When his phone rang, he nearly dropped it in his haste to answer.

"Hey, Rhy, what's up?" Maybe thinking of his boss had somehow garnered the call. "Did the Brookland PD give you any intel?"

"They have an ID on a print found in the homeowner's office," Rhy said. "I need you to put the phone on speaker so I can include Taylor in this discussion too."

"Yep, hang on." He lowered the device, pressed the speaker icon, and set it on the table. "Taylor, Rhy has information for us."

"Hi, Rhy," Taylor said. "I hope you have good news."

"Hi, Taylor, first I want to say I'm sorry you've had to go through this. I'm sure it hasn't been easy."

"Thank you." Taylor looked at Flynn as she spoke. "I'm blessed to have Flynn here protecting me."

"Flynn and the other members of our team will do everything we can to keep you safe," Rhy said. "As I was telling Flynn, they ran a partial print from Steve Miller's office. The print matches a man by the name of Roman Paulson."

The name meant nothing to Flynn, but based on the blood leeching from Taylor's features, she recognized it. Then he belatedly remembered the background check he'd done on Taylor back when he'd first joined forces with Zeke to keep Sienna and Bailey safe.

Paulson was Taylor's mother's maiden name.

CHAPTER FOUR

Taylor couldn't believe what she'd heard. Swallowing hard against the lump lodged in the back of her throat, she forced herself to respond. "Roman is one of my cousins on my mother's side. Her maiden name was Paulson."

"Does he look anything like the man you saw last night?" Rhy asked.

She tried to picture Roman as the gunman. She couldn't make the two memories mesh. She slowly shook her head. "No, but I haven't seen Roman in years. My mom's side of the family hasn't really been that close." A wave of nausea hit hard at the thought of her own flesh and blood killing innocent people.

And then coming after her.

"I'm going to send Flynn a mug shot," Rhy said. "I want you to take a look at it."

Knowing that Roman had a mug shot and prints on file gave her another jolt. "What crime did he commit?"

"Assault and battery four years ago," Rhy said. "He pled guilty for a reduced sentence."

Had assault and battery led to committing cold-blooded

murder? It was difficult for her to fathom the leap, especially since her fleeting impression of the gunman was that he'd been emotionally detached from the act, as if he killed people in their bed every day.

What had Flynn called it? A professional hit?

Flynn's phone dinged, and he took a moment to enlarge the photograph. He turned the phone so she could see the screen. "Try to imagine him with a beard."

The nose was wrong. She wasn't sure if she should be relieved or upset by the knowledge. "It's not him. The man I saw had a prominent nose. It was the first thing I noticed about him. Well, that and the fact that he'd killed two people."

"Okay, thanks for checking him out. Can you tell me anything else about your cousin? Any idea why he'd be meeting with Steve Miller?"

She sat back in her seat. The news of her cousin's fingerprint being found seemed anticlimactic if he wasn't the killer. "My mom mentioned that her second cousins Steve and Robin Miller needed a nanny. I knew there was a family relationship when I took the job, but I had never met them before. I believe Robin's mother, Sue, was my mother's cousin." It sounded convoluted even to her own ears. "My mother's brother, Donald Paulson, had three boys, Roman, Jake, and Lyle. But then Don and his wife got divorced, and the boys ended up living primarily with their mom, so we didn't see them much over the next few years. I guess that would make Roman, Jake, and Lyle second cousins to Robin, too, right?"

"That sounds correct," Rhy said thoughtfully. "So it could just be that Roman wanted to do his banking with his second cousin Steve."

"I guess so. Although I'm not sure why a meeting is

necessary." She glanced at Flynn. "I haven't met the president of the bank where I keep my money."

"I used to use Brookland Bank," Rhy said. "After my parents died, I ended up moving our account to a credit union to avoid extra banking fees. Back then, we needed every dime. I agree with you, Taylor. I never met with the president of the bank or the credit union."

"Is the fingerprint enough for a search warrant?" Flynn asked. "Maybe Roman has shady friends who are money laundering through the Brookland Bank."

"I thought of that possibility," Rhy said. "But his print isn't enough for probable cause. Especially since Taylor is convinced that he's not the shooter. Plus, there is a family connection, which may not be suspicious."

She tried to ignore the flash of guilt. She was being honest and answering questions to the best of her ability. She couldn't lie just to help with the investigation. Especially if her cousin's presence in the house was innocent. The more she considered the possibility of money laundering, the more ridiculous it sounded. "Maybe Roman needed a business loan and was having trouble getting one because of his criminal record." She looked from the phone screen to Flynn. "He may not be involved in the murders at all."

"Don't worry, we're keeping all possibilities open," Rhy said reassuringly. "No one wants to railroad your family member into being arrested for a crime he didn't commit. It's just one theory out of many. Our goal is to uncover the truth."

When she frowned, Flynn nodded. "Cops tend to take the position that everyone is a suspect until cleared. But that alone isn't enough for a judge to grant a search warrant. You make a good point about the possibility of your cousin looking for a loan. That's something we might be able to find without a search warrant."

She was surprised by his comment and hoped she was right about her cousin Roman. It wasn't good that he had a criminal record for assault and battery. Yet she wanted to believe that Roman had accepted responsibility for his actions and had turned his life around.

"Did the police in Brookland find anything else?" she asked, changing the subject from her cousin's guilt to the larger investigation.

"Not yet, the house was recently cleaned, and therefore they'd really focused on the fingerprint found in the office." Rhy sighed. "I wish I could say they found more evidence, but they haven't."

"I'll dig into Roman Paulson, see if I can find anything interesting there," Flynn offered. "Taylor is going through more mug shots."

"That's helpful, thanks. Stay focused on the guy's prominent nose rather than the beard," Rhy suggested.

"I have been trying to focus on the gunman's nose," Taylor said, trying not to sound annoyed. "I understand a beard can be shaved off."

"Okay, keep me updated on your progress," Rhy said. "I'll let Detective Klem know that Roman isn't the killer."

"Wait, Rhy? What about Max? Did the Brookland PD say anything about the little boy's foster family?"

"I'm not sure they'll be kept in the loop on that," Rhy said. "Once CPS takes over, police involvement ends. The only reason they'd stay in touch is if the child was a witness to a crime."

"Okay. Thanks." She knew she needed to let her concerns over Max's future go. Especially now that she had been targeted by the gunman too. But she couldn't help thinking about the little boy. He was such a sweetheart, just starting to smile and coo.

Enough. She couldn't dwell on Max's future. Not when there were bigger issues facing them.

Like a brutal killer intent on finding her.

She turned back to the computer, then paused. "Would you rather start digging into Roman Paulson's background?"

"No, Cass will hopefully be here soon." He glanced at his watch. "I'll make another pot of coffee while I wait."

She nodded, turning her gaze back to the computer screen. As slow and painstaking as it was, she was determined to do her part. If the gunman was somewhere in the police database, then she intended to find him.

Still, with each passing photo, her spirits flagged. She had to force herself to concentrate on the photos, not the possibility of her cousin Roman being involved in a plot to kill Steve and Robin Miller.

Once the coffee was brewed, Flynn refilled her cup and his own too. He settled in beside her and sipped his coffee while watching her work.

It was even more nerve-racking to scroll through one photo after another with Flynn so close. She caught a whiff of his woodsy scent, which brought another wave of awareness coursing through her.

Despite their differences—in personality and age—there was no denying the attraction simmering between them. On her part, not his. He'd looked down at her, which had made her angry.

She told herself his opinion of her career choice didn't matter. Sure, Flynn had a very important job. She hadn't been exposed to cops on a personal level until last month when Sienna had reached out to Zeke for protection.

It occurred to her that every face she clicked through on

the computer screen belonged to a criminal who had been arrested by a cop just like Flynn. His dedication to serving the public, to taking criminals off the street, was honorable.

She didn't like feeling as if she'd taken the easy way out by becoming a nanny.

Flynn's phone vibrated on the table. She glanced at him as he picked it up. "Cassidy and Jina are on their way."

"Is Jina a cop too?"

"Yes, recently married to another cop." A wry smile tugged at the corner of his mouth. "Jina is a tough cookie and the team's sharpshooter."

More women doing admirable jobs, she thought as she clicked through another mug shot. No wonder Flynn had acted like being a nanny was silly. "I'm sure it's harder for women to be taken seriously as police officers."

"Yeah, some guys tend to underestimate them." Flynn rose to refill his coffee. "Those of us on the tactical team use that to our advantage when we can. The most important thing of all is to have a cohesive team of skilled and competent cops to call on when a difficult job needs to be done."

She had noticed the camaraderie between Flynn, Zeke, and some of the other team members. Very different from what she was used to. Being a nanny was a solo occupation. Her interactions were primarily with kids and their parents.

And in some cases, she hadn't much liked the kids' parents.

Not that she was interested in changing careers at this point. Unless it was to follow her dream of being a writer. For now, her writing was more of a hobby. But maybe someday . . .

"Looks like Cass and Jina are in the neighborhood." Flynn set his coffee down and moved toward the side garage door. "I'm going to open the garage door, so Cass can park the rental inside."

"Sure thing." She managed a smile as Flynn disappeared into the garage. With a sigh, she turned her attention back to the mug shots. She was up to the letter *L* now, and not feeling as if this task was worthwhile.

Then again, it would be her luck that the killer was a guy with a last name that started with the letter *Z*. Ziegler or Zilke. She stared at one nose in a profile view after another, clicking through the photos as the garage door rumbled open.

Realizing her coffee cup was empty, she stood to cross over to the kitchen counter. The window over the sink overlooked the street. Two black SUVs pulled into the driveway, one going all the way up into the garage, the other stopping a few feet behind the first one.

A beautiful blonde emerged from the driver's seat. Jina, Taylor assumed, as she had met the red-haired Cassidy before.

No wonder Flynn had looked at her with disdain. He worked with smart, talented, and beautiful women who could hold their own on the street.

Her area of expertise was changing diapers.

While she stood there feeling inept, she noticed another black SUV coming down the street. She'd expected that to be another of Flynn's teammates, but the vehicle kept going. The garage door opened, and Flynn walked in with Cassidy.

"Hi, Taylor," Cassidy said. "I hear you've landed in a tough situation."

"That's one way of putting it," she said, offering a smile. "Nice to see you again."

Cassidy set the laptop case on the table, then tossed a

key fob to Flynn. "Computer and car as requested. Oh, and Rhy insisted I bring you extra cash too." She dug a wad of money from her pocket and set that on the table next to the computer. "Anything else?"

"No, I think I can handle things from here." Flynn reached for the cash. "Thanks for this, it will help us stay off-grid."

Cassidy frowned. "Do you need groceries?"

Flynn hesitated, then shook his head. "We should be fine for a day or two. If it takes longer than that, maybe."

"Okay, let me know." Cassidy glanced at the open laptop. "Mug shots, huh?"

"Yes. I'm looking for a very distinctive nose." She sighed. "So far I've come up empty-handed."

"You're assuming the killer is in the system," Cassidy said. She frowned at Flynn. "What if he's not a US citizen? If he's a professional hit man, he could be from Europe, Ireland, Australia—the possibilities are endless."

"Thanks, Cass, that's really helpful," Flynn said sarcastically. "We're working with what we have, which unfortunately isn't a lot."

"Sorry." Cassidy didn't sound the least bit apologetic. "I'll leave you to it. Call if you need anything else."

Flynn followed Cassidy outside, leaving Taylor with the computer feeling even more useless than ever before.

She had a feeling it was going to be a long day.

FLYNN STEPPED BACK in the garage after Cass and Jina had left. He should have thought about providing them with a grocery list, but it was too late now.

He could blame the situation, but that was no excuse.

He needed to keep his head screwed on straight. He'd spent a few days with Taylor last month. She had taken care of Bailey, which had helped put distance between them. And when she wasn't caring for Bailey, she was in her room scribbling in a notebook or typing on her tablet.

Now they were together again, without the distraction of a baby. Taylor dominated his thoughts and not in a good way.

He closed the garage door and headed back into the house. Having the second computer was a relief. He needed something to do, other than watching Taylor.

Maybe the discovery of Roman Paulson's fingerprint in Steve Miller's office was nothing important, but the only way to know that for sure was to dig into the guy's reasons for being there. Had it been a personal meeting or a business one? He wasn't as skilled as Gabe Melrose, the team's tech guru, but he figured he could handle a basic search.

Scouring social media sites had become common place in police work these days. Like every other cop he was acquainted with, he didn't personally use social media but had an anonymous profile page just for the purposes of digging into suspects.

A profile he planned to put to good use now.

As he logged into the precinct laptop, he caught Taylor's curious gaze. "What?"

"Nothing." She turned back to her screen. "I'm just—do you think Cassidy is right? That this gunman might not be from the US?"

"I don't honestly know what to think." He was irritated that Cass had mentioned it, but now he had to admit the bank angle was interesting. Maybe Steve Miller was somehow involved in money laundering. It could be the guy stumbled across something suspicious, which required the organized crime syndicate to take the drastic measure of killing him and his wife. But for now, he thought their time was best spent dealing with local possibilities. "Anything is possible. I'd still like you to keep going through mug shots, though."

"Yeah, I will." She turned back to her computer. "But I'm going to reach the end of the alphabet sooner or later. We'll need another plan by then."

"Maybe your cousin Roman Paulson will provide a lead." Even as he said the words, he knew Detectives Klem and Irving were probably paying Roman a visit. Flynn liked working for Rhy's tactical team, but there was something to be said for investigating a case.

Not that he had any plans to take the detective exam. He liked his job and the team.

He turned his attention to finding Roman Paulson on social media. Thankfully, the guy's name was unusual enough that he only had about ten profiles to sift through.

"Hey, Taylor? Is this your cousin?" He turned the screen to show her the profile that looked similar to the photograph Rhy had sent. "He has a five-o'clock shadow here, unlike his clean-shaven face on the mug shot."

"Yes, that looks like the guy in the picture, but like I told you, I haven't seen Roman in years." She leaned closer, then took over his keyboard. She tapped a few keys, and then said, "Yeah, I'm positive this is my cousin Roman. See here, his brothers Jake and Lyle are listed as his friends."

He quickly scrolled through to see the profile pictures of both Jake and Lyle Paulson. Then he turned the computer toward her again. "What do you think? Any chance one of these guys was the shooter?"

She frowned but took a moment to go through their photos. "They don't have the same nose."

He nodded, not surprised by her answer. It was worth a try. Then a thought occurred to him. "What about you?" He turned to face her. "You're related to these guys. Do you have a social media account?"

"I do, yes." She flushed as if embarrassed. "I don't post anything, though. What am I going to post about? I don't eat fancy food to take pictures of or hang out at gatherings with my friends. Even when I do those things, I'm not big into posting them online for everyone to see. I went through and took a lot of my old posts from college off my page when I decided to go the nanny route. I didn't want any potential parents looking at those old pictures and judging me unfairly."

"I totally agree with you. I don't use social media either, but that's more of a cop thing," he said. "I only asked because most people I know are on these sites."

"That's true, but as a nanny, I would never post photos of the kids I care for, that just seems to be asking for trouble."

"So why bother?" he asked.

She flushed. "I have an account in case I need one for marketing purposes if I ever get around to finishing and publishing my book." She looked away, as if embarrassed by her secret desire to be a published author.

"Ah, that makes sense." He remembered her dream was to write a book. "So you're not friends with Roman or his brothers."

"No, although to be honest, I haven't bothered to check my account recently." She frowned, then said, "I guess it's possible they've sent me a friend request that I'm unaware of. Did you want me to check on that?"

Flynn hesitated, torn between wanting Taylor to finish with the mug shots and getting access to her account. "Yes, if you could log into the social media site using this computer, that would be great."

"I'll try. But you know how it is with passwords. It's been so long I may have forgotten which one I used." She went through the motions of logging him out of the social media website, then attempted to log in as herself. Her first try was not successful. He wondered if there was a limit to how many times you could attempt to get in when she abruptly grinned. "I remembered! Here you go."

"Thanks." He figured it would be easier to look around as Taylor than as his anonymous account. For one thing, he noticed right away that Taylor was friends with her mother, who in turn was friends with her cousin Susan who was, of course, friends with her own daughter, Robin Miller. The family connection was right there in living color for the entire world to see.

If they bothered to look. Which made him fear the killer might in fact do just that.

He paused when he came across Robin Miller's smiling face beaming from the screen. Were they on the wrong track with focusing on her husband Steve Miller's banking background? Was it possible the double homicide was related to her interior design business? Hard to imagine how the task of picking out colors and types of furniture could lead to such a brutal crime, but Taylor had mentioned famous athletes. Money was at the root of many crimes.

He shrugged the remote possibility off. Robin's business would have to be considered, but for now, he decided to stick with Roman as the potential link to the shooter. The suspect being Taylor's cousin was an added complication.

One he couldn't ignore.

They worked side by side for a full hour before Taylor

pushed away from the table. "These faces are starting to blur together," she said with a sigh. "I need a break."

"Absolutely, take all the time you need." He glanced at her computer screen, noticing she'd gotten up to the letter S. She was doing a good job of getting through the mug shots, but the longer it took, the less likely they'd find their perp in the system.

He believed Taylor would know the guy when she saw him. She'd seemed very sure of the guy's larger than normal nose.

But she wasn't trained in surveillance either. It had been a brief glimpse as the guy walked past while she was scared to death.

Even a seasoned cop could make a mistake in identifying a suspect under those conditions.

"Flynn?" Her voice was underlined with a sense of urgency. "I think this is the same car that drove past earlier when Cass and Jina came."

"What car?" He shot to his feet and rushed over to where she stood at the kitchen sink. Was it possible Cass or Jina had been followed here?

"That black SUV," she said, indicating the vehicle that was already disappearing from view. "I remember thinking there was a third member of the team, but it went past, so I assumed it belonged to one of the neighbors."

"Grab the computers," he said in a terse voice. He thumbed the phone screen to call Cass. "Any chance you were followed here?"

"What? No, we backtracked to make sure we weren't," Cassidy said. "Why, what's going on?"

He hesitated, wondering if he was overreacting. "Taylor noticed a black SUV going past when you guys arrived.

And another black SUV just drove past again. I don't like it."

"Get out of there," Cass advised. "I'll come out to meet you. I already dropped Jina off at the precinct."

"Yeah, that works." He told himself it was better to err on the side of caution. "I'll be in touch."

Shoving the phone in his pocket, he took the two stacked laptops from Taylor's hands. "Let's go. We're taking the rental, which is in the bay farthest from the door."

She nodded, but then said, "I could be wrong, Flynn. I'm not a car expert. I just remembered thinking that three black SUVs were strange."

"Cass doesn't think she was followed, but I'd rather hit the road than be a sitting duck." He tucked the computers under one arm, then reached for the door handle with the other.

A crack of gunfire on the heels of shattering glass from the broken kitchen window had him throwing himself toward Taylor. "Down!" he shouted hoarsely.

She let out a muffled *oomph* as the laptop computers knocked into her. He let them fall to the floor in a loud thud to reach for his weapon.

He kicked himself for being too slow. He should have gotten Taylor out of there right away, without calling Cassidy.

Now he was very much afraid it might be too late.

CHAPTER FIVE

Huddling on her hands and knees below the kitchen counter, Taylor realized she wasn't nearly as afraid of being next to Flynn as she had been the night of the murders. For one thing, she wasn't holding an innocent baby whose life depended on her. Even better, she wasn't alone in the middle of the night. There was something to be said for having a cop at her side.

Then a second gunshot punctured the window, making her put her hands over her head as if they could actually stop a bullet from killing her. Not even close. It occurred to her that if Flynn was hit, the gunman would be able to finish her off without a problem.

"Come with me," Flynn said. "We need to get into the garage."

"Okay." This wasn't the time to argue. The laptops were on the floor beside her. She quickly gathered them up and rose into a crouch, doing her best to keep her head down and out of the line of fire. When Flynn gave her a nudge, she made her way toward the doorway leading to the attached garage. She had left her puffy coat on the chair and quickly snagged it. There wasn't time to grab anything else.

Flynn was right behind her. Tucking the coat under her arm, she opened the door and crossed the threshold, standing upright as she did so. But there wasn't time to revel in their relative safety. The gunman may have assumed they'd gone this way and start peppering the garage door with bullets.

As if reading her mind, Flynn said, "Hurry. We need to get out of here."

The garage wasn't that big, so making their way around the first SUV that belonged to Flynn to reach the second one meant scooting through the narrow gap. Her coat dragged along the side of the car, the laptops growing heavy in her arms. When she finally reached the passenger-side door, she dumped the computers on the floor. Then she drew on her coat before settling into the seat.

Flynn was already behind the wheel. He hesitated for a moment, glancing at her. "He's likely to shoot the garage door when I start the car. Keep your head down, okay?"

She grabbed his arm. "Maybe we should wait. One of the neighbors must have called the police by now."

"Cassidy is on her way back—" He was interrupted by the sound of gunfire pummeling the garage door. Thankfully, it wasn't the one they were sitting behind, but the one where his car was located. "Time's up. We gotta move."

Whispering a silent prayer, she released Flynn's arm and bent over in the passenger seat. She brought the edges of her coat up to muffle her need to scream. He started the engine, threw the gearshift into reverse, and slammed the rear of the car through the aluminum garage door. There was a shriek of metal against metal as he pushed through the door.

Somehow, they were out of the garage and moving backward down the driveway. Taylor expected to hear more gunfire, but she only heard the distinct wail of police sirens. The wave of relief was dizzying.

But their situation was still grim. Flynn finally hit the brake when they reached the road, put the car into drive, and rolled down the street. She gingerly lifted her head, noticing he was going in the same direction as the black SUV had gone.

Was he hoping to catch up with the gunman? Swallowing hard, she gripped the handrest and braced herself. While she wanted nothing more than to find this guy, she felt as if they were at a disadvantage.

Flynn was armed, but he was also driving. If they'd been thinking clearly, he would have put her in the driver's seat.

Not that she'd have been brave enough to ram through the closed garage door.

"Where are we going?" She forced the question past her tight throat.

"Catching up to Cassidy, hopefully." He pulled his phone from his pocket and thumbed the screen. Then he handed it to her. "She's my most recent call."

"I see it." She quickly pressed on her name to make the call, quickly placing the phone on speaker.

"Flynn, where are you?" Cassidy asked, her tone urgent.

"We're out of Zeke's place, on the road in the rental," Flynn said. "The back of the vehicle is probably damaged after the way I went through the garage door. It's compromised anyway, so we need a new ride."

There was a slight pause before Cassidy spoke. "Okay, I'm halfway to Zeke's place myself but let's reconvene at the rental car agency in Brookland. If you can make it that far."

"We'll make it." Flynn's tone was grim. "I haven't seen the black SUV, at least not yet. I am concerned about how this guy found us. I doubt he followed you, so that means he must have known we were hanging out at Zeke's place. Maybe he has police connections providing key information on members of our team."

"That's possible," Cass said. "If that's true, we need to find a place for you and Taylor to stay that is not affiliated with the team in any way."

"I agree. Going to the rental agency in Brookland is not an option," Flynn said. "I'll head to the airport instead."

"That's not a bad idea." There was a brief pause, then Cassidy added, "I'll meet you and Taylor there."

"Thanks." Flynn glanced at her as she held the phone between them. "We'll see you soon." He gave her a nod, indicating she could disconnect from the call. She dropped the device into the center console cupholder between them.

"You really believe the gunman has police connections?" She couldn't hide her shock.

"I don't know what to think," Flynn said. "Other than we should have been safe at Zeke's place. But we weren't." He looked as if he wanted to say more but didn't.

She dragged her shaking fingers through her hair, trying to understand. "Maybe Cassidy and Jina were followed. I saw the SUV pretty quickly after they arrived. Like I said, I thought the car was being driven by another of your teammates."

"That's just it. Cassidy and Jina are seasoned cops; they know how to spot a tail." He shook his head. "No way they'd have missed it. If you saw the black SUV coming down the road that quickly after their arrival, I think it's more likely the gunman just happened to show up as they did. Only he kept driving past the house because he was seriously outnumbered three cops to one. After biding his time, he returned when he assumed we were alone."

What Flynn said made sense. What did she know? This was all far outside her area of expertise. She glanced up at the gray-cloud-covered November sky as he headed toward the interstate. She'd been to the airport numerous times, but not for the sole reason of obtaining a rental car. "I don't understand why he'd come after me in broad daylight."

Flynn's expression hardened. "I believe he saw you through the kitchen window and decided to take the shot. Once he did that, he was committed to seeing it through. Until he realized the cops were on the way."

She shivered, imagining the big-nosed man pointing his weapon at her and pulling the trigger. Frustrating that she hadn't gotten a better look at him. As she'd gone through one mug shot after another, she'd feared her memory wasn't as accurate as she'd hoped. What if she'd made his nose larger in her mind than it was? She didn't know much about the psychology of trauma, but it wasn't a stretch to believe being scared out of her mind had altered her senses.

Making things look different from reality.

"It's okay," Flynn said, reaching for her hand. He had relaxed a bit now that they were far from Zeke's home. She'd noticed he'd watched the rearview mirror like a hawk, but it seemed they may have escaped the gunman. At least, this time. "Don't worry. I'm not going to let him get close to you."

"I trust you." She tried to smile. "You've saved my life twice now. I'm not sure how I'll every repay you."

He frowned. "No payment is necessary. Protecting the

innocent is what we do. There's no quid pro quo here. Just a friend helping out a friend."

Friends. She hadn't viewed Flynn as a friend when he'd first arrived at the hotel to keep her and Sienna's daughter, Bailey, safe. Just the opposite as he'd seemed to look down at her. Yet that knowledge hadn't stopped her from reaching out to him when the Millers were murdered. Maybe she needed to lighten up a bit. He was a nice guy and genuinely wanted to help.

She nodded, giving his hand a squeeze. "Thanks for being my friend."

"Anytime." He held her hand for a moment longer, then released it. She told herself he was just being nice, but once again, she sensed that weird awareness shimmering between them.

Most likely it was her imagination. She was letting her gratitude toward Flynn mess with her mind. She was leaning on him in a way she'd never depended on anyone else. But as he'd made it clear, they were friends.

Nothing more.

She didn't say anything as the airport exit came into view. Flynn had made good time on the expressway. The morning rush was over, so the roads weren't too crowded. Still, she found herself watching the cars around them, half expecting to see the black SUV being driven by a man with a gun.

"You mentioned he was a professional hit man," she said, breaking the silence. "The man who fired at us at Zeke's didn't come across as a professional."

"That's true." He shot her a quick glance. "I think he acted impulsively. Maybe overestimating his skill at hitting his target. But you have a point that the man in the black SUV could be someone else."

"What?" She stared at him. "I didn't say that."

"You pointed out the differences in the two attempts. The gunman at the Miller home was brutal and methodical. The shots fired from the black SUV were not." He shrugged. "Something to consider."

"I can't see why anyone else would be involved in trying to shoot me." The thought of more than one gunman coming after her was mind-boggling.

"You're missing the point of a professional hit," Flynn said gently. "The professional is hired by someone else to do the dirty work. That same person can hire as many gunmen as he wants to get the job done."

An icy chill washed over her. Because he was right. She hadn't thought of the situation from that perspective. She'd assumed that the gunman who'd killed the Millers had come after her of his own accord because she had seen him. Because he had been forced to let her slip away.

But maybe the person who'd hired the gunman was the one who wanted her dead.

If she and Max had been asleep in their respective beds, she had no doubt that they would have been shot and killed.

Just like the Millers.

And she still had no idea why any of this was happening.

AS TAYLOR TWISTED her fingers together in her lap, her expression a frozen mask of fear, Flynn realized he shouldn't have been so blunt. Yet he couldn't keep her in the dark about the extent of the threat against her.

Not after the way they'd been found at Zeke's.

He needed to find a way to reassure her, but that wasn't

easy to do when he was kicking himself for being an idiot. He shouldn't have used his best friend's home as a hiding spot.

Hadn't he learned anything from the way his teammates had been in trouble over the past year? Sure, he and others had stepped in to help each other out when danger lurked nearby. But they had stayed in motels or rental properties. Even the MPD safe house.

They had not gone and stayed in each other's homes.

He needed to think about how to best keep Taylor safe while at the same time figure out who was behind these attacks. Because somehow he didn't have much faith in the ability of the Brookland detectives to get to the bottom of this mess.

He entered the airport parking structure, taking note of the sign indicating which levels still had parking spots available. Milwaukee had grown over the past few years such that the airport was seeing a huge increase in visitors coming and going.

The fourth level seemed to have the most open spots, so he got off on that floor and began driving up and down the aisles. He pulled into an open spot in the back row, then threw the gearshift into park and killed the engine.

"Now what?" Taylor's voice was full of apprehension. "Do we wait here for Cassidy?"

"Yes. When we know she's here, we'll go inside and get a rental car." He smiled reassuringly. "Then we'll work out our next steps."

She gave a slight nod, settling back in the seat. He was glad she'd grabbed her winter coat on the way out of Zeke's place. He only had his fleece, but that was okay.

He'd rather not be hampered by a bulky winter coat.

They sat in silence for several long minutes. When his

phone jangled in the cupholder, he grabbed it. "Hey, Cass, where are you?"

"Pulling up to the airport parking lot now," she said. "What floor are you on?"

"Fourth floor." He gave her the corresponding color and aisle. "See you soon."

"Yep." She ended the call.

Five minutes later, Cassidy pulled up beside them.

"There she is. Let's go," he said.

Taylor opened her car door, then gestured to the laptops on the floor at her feet. "I take it we should bring the computers?"

"Yes." He took a moment to tuck his handgun out of sight beneath his fleece, then bent over to scoop them up. It wasn't like he could walk into the airport holding a gun in his hand. Even having one on his person was risky. But they wouldn't be there too long, and technically the car rentals were just outside the airport proper. "I've got them."

"Whoa, Flynn, that's worse than I imagined." Cassidy winced as she stood staring at the damaged back end of the SUV. "Rhy isn't going to be happy when that repair bill hits his budget."

He felt bad about that, their team had caused a lot of damage to cars and hotel rooms over the past eleven months, but there hadn't been much of a choice. "Assistant Chief Michaels is the one who will be mad. Rhy understands."

"Yeah, but"—Cass stopped, then shrugged—"never mind. I guess there's nothing we can do about it now."

"The police department pays for that?" Taylor asked, eyeing the damage with a mixture of shock and horror. "I'm surprised."

"Well, the good news is that we always pay for the additional insurance up front when we rent cars," Cassidy said with a wry grin. "That has helped to keep the costs down."

Hating the thought of failing Rhy and the rest of the team by causing trouble, Flynn swallowed against the lump in his throat. He'd often felt like the weak link in the team, and this latest incident was not helping. He forced himself to turn his back on the damaged rental. "Let's go." He gestured toward the yellow walkway that several other airport goers were using to go from one end of the structure to the other. "The sooner we get a rental car and get out of here, the better."

"Hey, I was only kidding about Rhy," Cassidy said, falling into step beside him. "He won't blame you."

"Maybe he should." The comment popped out of his mouth before he could stop it. "I made a stupid mistake in going to Zeke's."

"Funny, but I don't think Rhy viewed it that way. And neither did me and Jina," Cass added. "We can't predict every move the bad guys make. If we could, we'd be able to solve crimes before they happened."

He appreciated her attempt to make him feel better, but it wasn't working. Time to change the subject. "I was thinking of booking a rental property through one of those home-share services rather than using another hotel. We've burned our bridges at both the American Lodge and the City Central Hotel."

"Timberland Falls Suites too," Cass agreed. "Although in all fairness, we never caused any room damage at Timberland Falls. Just a few bullet holes in the door of the front lobby, which is nothing compared to the damage we've caused elsewhere."

Taylor turned to look at him. "Seriously?"

"Yeah, it's not as bad as it sounds." He elbowed Cass in

the ribs to shut her up. Everything Cass said was true, but Taylor didn't need to hear it. Especially the part where bullets had been embedded in the door. He squelched another flash of guilt over the broken window and garage door of Zeke's home. Considering the winter chill, he needed to figure out how to get them repaired.

One problem at a time, he thought grimly.

"Don't worry, we'll find a place to keep you safe," Cass said, apparently realizing how concerned Taylor was.

They spent the rest of the trip to the airport rental car station in silence. Flynn was trying to figure out how he could rent the car without using his name, or even Cassidy's. Even using one of their names on the rental property might bring trouble.

But what option did he have? Fake IDs came in handy on TV, but they weren't readily available in real life.

They stood in line, waiting for their turn. When a clerk gestured them forward, Cassidy moved forward, putting a hand on his arm. "I've got this. I spoke with Gabe. We've already reserved a rental under his name."

"Gabe agreed to that?" He was surprised to hear Gabe Melrose, the tactical team's tech expert, was willing to go out on a limb.

"Yes. After all, you mentioned that the gunman might have connections to find the names of our tactical team. But Gabe works behind the scenes." She smiled. "His name isn't out in the limelight like ours have been."

That was true. "Okay, that works. Tell him thanks."

"Tell him yourself," she shot back, then walked up to the counter. "I'd like to pick up an SUV under the name of Gabe Melrose."

It didn't take long for them to sign the paperwork. Then they headed back outside to pick up the car.

"Sorry, it's silver instead of black," Cassidy said. "But that may help. The gunman isn't going to expect you to be in a light-colored vehicle."

Flynn tried not to think about how easy it would be to hit the silver SUV in the darkness. Then he thrust that depressing thought aside. If they'd covered their tracks well enough by using Gabe's name, then the color of the SUV wouldn't be a problem.

He hoped.

"I'm sure I can convince Gabe to rent a house for you too," Cass was saying as he dropped the laptops on the floor of the back seat. "You can drop me off at the precinct, then head out to whichever property you choose."

"Sounds good." He forced himself to sound confident and upbeat for Taylor's sake. "Let's hit the road."

Taylor was unusually quiet as he left the rental car agency. She'd taken the back seat, leaving Cass to sit up front. He glanced at her through the rearview mirror. "Are you okay?" he finally asked.

"Yes." The way she turned her head to gaze out the window belied her words. She didn't look fine. And how could he blame her?

She was likely losing faith in him. He'd really botched his last attempt to keep her safe. She had been the one to alert him to the black SUV that she had seen driving by twice. Something he'd failed to notice.

Kicking himself wasn't going to help. All he could do was to move forward with the next phase of their plan.

And using Gabe's name might be the extra safety net they needed.

"I need you to help me get Zeke's window repaired," he said to Cass. "His garage doors too. The gunman fired rounds at the one garage door, and we busted the second one. I don't want kids getting inside and ransacking the place."

"Sure. I'll get Steele and Brock to help with that. They'll have to coordinate with the Greenland PD anyway to make sure they get all the evidence collected. Maybe we'll get a match on the ballistics, linking the weapon to the gun used in the double homicide." She worked her phone with her thumbs, clearly sending text messages. "Any idea when Zeke, Sienna, and Bailey will be back?"

"No clue. I guess they're in Hot Springs, Arkansas, for her tour." He had to think for a moment about what day of the week it was. "Today is Thursday, so I'm sure they won't be back until Monday at the earliest."

"Got it." Cass continued to look down at her phone. "Sounds like Steele and Brock are available and willing to help."

"Good." Some of the despair he'd been feeling eased from his shoulders. Bad enough that he'd almost gotten Taylor killed. He didn't want to leave Zeke, Sienna, and Bailey in the lurch.

"I'm glad Sienna and Zeke are out of town," Taylor said. "I don't think they should return to the house until the gunman has been caught." She paused, then added, "If he's caught."

"Good point. Once we're settled in a safe location, I'll fill Zeke in on what happened." He caught her gaze in the mirror. "And we will get this guy."

Again, she didn't look convinced.

When he reached their seventh district police station, he drove around back to park out of sight. There's no way the gunman could have tracked them this quickly, but he was done with taking chances.

He led the way to the side door, holding it for Cass and Taylor.

When they were safely inside the building, he brushed past the women and headed straight for Rhy's office. "We were found at Zeke's home, and I damaged another rental."

Rhy arched a brow. "Oh yeah? We got the insurance on it, right?"

"Yes. I believe so." He waited for Rhy to yell at him, but he should have known better.

"It was bound to happen sooner or later," Rhy said with a shrug. "We were on a good streak there for a while. The good news is that we've put a lot of bad men and women behind bars. Michaels gives us extra brownie points for that."

He was humbled by Rhy's support. "That's true. And I would like nothing better than to add this gunman to the list. I'm concerned about what connections he has," Flynn said. "It's like he has inside information on me and the other members of the tactical team."

Rhy nodded slowly. "I can understand your concern. You think there might be a Brookland cop on his payroll?"

"More like on the payroll of the man who'd hired the hit man in the first place," Flynn said. "I keep going back to how Steve Miller is the president of a bank. And that he'd met with Taylor's cousin in his office shortly before the murders."

"No luck on the mug shots yet?" Rhy asked.

"No. Taylor is doing her best, but I'm starting to think this guy isn't in the system." He hesitated, then asked, "Have you gotten any new information from the Brookland PD?"

As Rhy shook his head, the phone on his desk rang.

Arching a brow, he reached for the handset. "Captain Finnegan."

Flynn was about to step away to give his boss privacy, but Rhy gestured for him to stay. "Yes, Detective Klem. I would love an update on your case."

Flynn wished the call was on speaker but managed to hold back from pushing the button himself. Rhy's expression turned somber. "I see. Yes, that's very unfortunate. Thank you for the update."

"What's unfortunate?" He stared at Rhy as he replaced the receiver. "Something bad happened."

"Yes. It appears Roman Paulson was murdered. Shot at close range with two bullets to the center of his chest." Rhy held his gaze, then sighed. "Just like the Millers."

That wasn't good. The gunman was eliminating any potential loose ends related to the double homicide.

And Taylor was likely the biggest loose end of all.

CHAPTER SIX

Cassidy gestured to a chair at one of the cubicle stations. "Have a seat. Would you like water or coffee? Fair warning on the latter, it may taste like scorched earth."

Taylor managed a weak smile. "Water would be good, thanks."

Cassidy headed for a doorway off to the side, likely some sort of break room. Back when she'd been teaching at the day care, they'd had a similar space.

She wondered where Flynn was. He had veered away from her and Cassidy the moment they'd gotten inside the building. She knew he felt guilty for the way they'd been found at Zeke's house, but it wasn't his fault.

After all, she was the sole reason Flynn was in danger. She'd called him after hearing the shots and catching a glimpse of the gunman. If Flynn hadn't taken her under his wing, she'd probably be already dead.

"Here you go." Cassidy returned with a bottle of water. Taylor took a long, grateful sip. Her nerves weren't cut out for this kind of thing. Her hands were still trembling, despite being safe in the precinct.

Maybe she should ask Flynn if they could simply live in the police station. She couldn't think of a better place to stay.

"It's going to be okay," Cassidy said, echoing the words Flynn had been telling her from the beginning of this nightmare. "Flynn is a good cop and determined to protect you. He'll do whatever it takes."

"I know." She didn't doubt Flynn's dedication to his job and to keeping her safe. She eyed the pretty redhead curiously. "How do you like being a cop?"

"I love it." Cassidy smiled, but then her expression sobered. "It's not for everyone. I see the worst side of human nature more times than I care to. Sometimes it's hard to keep the faith. To continuously strive for justice."

The profile of the gunman with his prominent nose flashed in her mind. Only a truly evil man could shoot people in cold blood while they slept. She hadn't realized how often the police encountered bad guys with no moral compass.

"I can't imagine how you and Flynn and everyone else stays strong," she admitted. "Caring for young kids can be a challenge, but they are mostly sweet, honest, and kind." She had noticed that kids absorbed their personalities from their parents, though. She'd had one job where the kids treated her terribly because that was how the parents acted toward her.

"Speaking of Flynn, there he is now." Cassidy nodded toward her fellow cop. "I'll check in on Gabe, see if he's found any rental properties close by."

Taylor nodded, but her gaze was riveted on Flynn's somber features. Feeling shaky, she rose to her feet. "What is it? You look like you've gotten bad news."

He came closer and reached for her hand. "I'm sorry,

Taylor. But your cousin Roman Paulson was found dead in his home by the local police."

What? Roman was dead? She frowned. "I don't understand. He's only a few years older than I am." Then she understood. "He was murdered? You're telling me my cousin has been murdered?"

"Yes, shot twice in the chest at close range." Flynn held her gaze. "There was no forced entry to his home, so the working theory is that Roman knew the man who'd killed him."

Again, the prominent nose profile flashed in her mind. "Roman was involved in this somehow."

"Yes, we believe so." Flynn gently squeezed her hand. "I'm sorry I don't have better news for you."

Clinging to Flynn's hand, she tried to digest the information. She felt bad about Roman. Even if he had been involved in something illegal, he didn't deserve to be murdered.

First Steve and Robin Miller, now Roman. How many more people would lose their lives over—whatever this was?

Not Flynn, Lord. Please not Flynn!

It was horrible to be the one targeted by a gunman, but she wasn't sure she could handle other innocent people losing their lives in an effort to protect her.

Especially Flynn.

"Maybe I need to go away. Like out of state." She didn't have a lot of money in her bank account, most of her nanny income was centered on paying off her student loans. "Far away where this guy will never find me."

"I understand why you would think that, Taylor." Flynn's voice was soft but held a note of urgency. "But it's not a practical solution. You'd have to find a job, which would lead the killer right back to you. It's not easy to stay completely off-grid, but we'll find a way to do that here where we can protect you."

She shook her head, more because she didn't like what he was saying. And suddenly she was mad. "I hate this." The words burst from her throat. "I hate that this guy is looking for me! That he wants to kill me!"

"I know." Flynn drew her into his arms. "I don't blame you. I'm not happy about this either."

His calm demeanor wasn't helping. She wanted to punch someone, preferably the big-nosed man, but of course, that was a foolish thought.

Blowing out a heavy sigh, she relaxed against Flynn, absorbing his strength. She knew running away wasn't the answer, no matter how tempting. "I don't want you to get hurt," she whispered against him.

"I won't." He surprised her by pressing a quick kiss to her temple. "Don't worry about me. We'll get through this."

She desperately wanted to believe that. But thinking back to how things had gone with Sienna, how she'd been kidnapped and Zeke had been shot while trying to save her, wasn't reassuring.

As terrible as that situation had been for them, it wasn't close to the one she faced now. The man hunting her had no heart and the soul of the devil. He seemed intent on letting nothing get in the way of killing her.

And as things stood, there was little hope of finding him.

"Flynn?" Cassidy's voice penetrated her thoughts. She drew in one last breath, filling her senses with Flynn's scent, then pushed away. Her knees wobbled a bit, but she managed to stay upright under her own power.

"Did you talk to Gabe?" Flynn asked. He kept a hand on the small of her back as if sensing she still needed support. Oddly, his sweet gesture made her eyes sting with tears.

She blinked them away, annoyed with herself. She might not be tough and strong like Jina and Cassidy, but it wasn't like her to cry over things either.

"Yes, why don't you come and see what your options are?" Cassidy gestured toward an office not far from the breakroom. "Gabe has identified a few possibilities."

"What about the safe house?" Flynn asked, gently urging her forward. Together they headed toward Gabe's small office. "We could really use those bullet-resistant windows as this guy seems to like taking shots at Taylor."

"Unfortunately, there's a family staying there." Cassidy grimaced as she made room for them to crowd around Gabe.

"Cass is right; the safe house is being used at the moment." Gabe turned in his chair to face them. "Hi, I'm Gabe Melrose. I hear you're in some trouble."

"Taylor Templeton," she said. "Yeah, trouble is one way to put it."

"Thanks for allowing us to use your name on the rental car and the property," Flynn added. "I owe you big time."

"Nah, it's the least I can do." Gabe waved that off. "Okay, I found three options. They're all relatively small homes, which are cheaper obviously than larger ones. I figure you would rather be outside the city limits with a little more space between the houses."

She had no idea if that was better for their needs or not, so she remained silent, letting Flynn take the lead.

"Right on all counts." Flynn leaned over to see the screen past Gabe's shoulder. The office might be small, but there were three computer monitors mounted on a frame on his desk.

"This one is in Timberland Falls." Gabe tapped one

screen. "I only included it because the price was so reasonable. I know you guys tend to avoid Timberland Falls."

"The cops weren't too bad when we worked with them last month," Flynn said with a shrug. "I think we're growing on them."

"Okay, so that's one option. Here's the second option, a two-bedroom house in Peabody. It's on the lake, but it's November, so the price is reasonable."

"Hmm. That's a good choice," Flynn said. "At least we'd be close to Jina's husband, Cole Roberts."

"Exactly what I thought," Gabe said with a grin. Then he tapped the keyboard bringing a third home up on the third screen. "This is the most expensive place. It's farther from other homes, though, so I figured you might like it. Oh, it's in White Gull Bay."

Any of the places looked more than reasonable to her. She'd probably choose the least expensive of the bunch, considering the damage to the rental car.

"I like the one on Peabody Lake," Flynn said. "It's not that much more than the place in Timberland Falls, and we have the added plus of friendly cops nearby if anything happens. Not that it will," he quickly said, darting a glance at her. "I'm sure we'll be fine."

"Whatever you think is best," she said with a shrug. "You're the expert."

"I like that one too," Cassidy said. "It's closer to Brookland, which might come in handy if the police need to talk to you again."

"I'll book it right now." Gabe hit a few keys, then glanced at his watch. "It's going to take a few minutes to hear back. It looks like the place is open now, so hopefully you can get in sooner than later."

"Understood. Thanks, Gabe." Flynn clapped him on the back. "You're the best."

Gabe blushed, darting a glance at Cassidy before turning back to his array of screens. "In the meantime, I've been trying to find intel on Roman Paulson. Rhy said he wanted to help Brookland PD on the case."

"Unfortunately, we recently learned Roman was murdered," Flynn said.

"Wow," Cassidy murmured. "That's not good."

"Tell me about it," Flynn said. "Check with Rhy, but I would still be interested to know what Roman was up to. We have to assume he was silenced for a reason."

"Maybe they should check in with his brothers, Lyle and Jake." Taylor wasn't sure why she didn't think of that earlier. "They might know what Roman was up to."

"I believe the detectives were headed there next," Flynn said. "Hopefully, they'll cooperate with the investigation."

A horrible thought struck, and she grabbed Flynn's arm. "Is my family in danger? My parents? My siblings? My parents are out of the country now, but what if the gunman tries to track them down? Should they be in a safe house too?"

"How long will your parents be on vacation?" Flynn asked.

"Another three and a half weeks. They're cruising Europe. I'm honestly not even sure where they are today." She felt like a lousy daughter for not knowing her parents' itinerary off the top of her head. "I can check my email. I have their schedule written down. My siblings are in college. One is in graduate school in Atlanta, and the other is a senior in Sacramento, on the West Coast."

"No need to check your email now." Flynn waved a hand. "If you don't know where your parents are, it's not likely the gunman will be able to track them down. And your siblings being in different states helps too. I can't imagine the killer would bother to track your family across the country or halfway around the globe. He only killed Roman because he was somehow involved in whatever is going on."

He was probably right. There was no reason to panic.

Still, she sent up a silent prayer for God to keep her parents and her siblings safe.

FLYNN DREW Taylor back to the cubicle where she'd left her half-finished water bottle. He hoped it wouldn't take long to make the arrangements with the rental property. Now that he had a destination in mind, he was anxious to get Taylor out there and settled in.

He was glad her parents were out of the country and her siblings were out of state. He hated to admit he should have considered her family's safety before now. If the gunman knew who Taylor was, he could easily find her parents and siblings.

Use them to flush Taylor out of hiding.

He sat on the edge of the desk, praying he hadn't forgotten anything else. He turned to face her. "Where do your parents live? Is anyone watching over your parents' house?"

"Their neighbor. I would have offered, but my schedule is dependent on what the Millers needed from me. Was dependent on that," she said sadly. "My parents live in Madison. Why?"

He considered that for a moment. Madison was seventy miles away, which meant it was not necessarily convenient to head over there. But it also wasn't too far to keep the gunman from heading over to check things out. Based on the recent activity here in town, he didn't think the gunman had made the trip. There hadn't been time for him to drive all the way out there, investigate if anyone was home, then return to the area.

He stood. "Hang on, I need to check with Rhy. He may know someone within the Madison PD who can do a drive-by past your parents' home. What's the address?"

There was a sticky-note pad on the desk. She quickly wrote down her parents' address on the white square. "Thanks, Flynn. I'll feel better knowing someone is going to keep an eye on the place while they're gone."

With a nod, he took the note to Rhy's office. If he remembered correctly, Roscoe's cousin Cameron Stevenson was a cop in Madison. He'd recently married his girlfriend, Jennifer. Flynn had covered Roscoe's weekend so he and Libby could attend the ceremony.

He tapped his knuckle on the doorframe. "Rhy? Have a minute?"

"Yeah." Rhy ran his fingers through his short blond hair. "I'm always happy for an excuse to avoid working on the budget."

He didn't envy his boss that task and felt guilty all over again regarding the damage to the rental SUV. He stepped in and set the sticky note on his desk. "Taylor is worried about her family. Her parents are in Europe, so it's not likely the killer will find them, but I was thinking we could contact Cam Stevenson to have him check out her parents' place. Make sure there's no one hanging around."

"I can do that. I'm sure Cam won't mind." Rhy picked up the sticky note. "I'm glad her parents are out of the country. That makes things easier for us."

"Yeah. Her sibs are out of state, too, at different colleges." He shrugged. "I'll pick up a disposable phone for Taylor so she can reach out to them, but I'm not sure it helps the killer to head out to Atlanta or Sacramento."

"Agreed." Rhy sat back in his chair. "I wish I knew what this was about. At this point, the Brookland PD doesn't have many leads. We're assuming something with the Brookland Bank, but that could be anything from money laundering to outstanding loans or even dabbling in cryptocurrency."

Flynn hadn't considered cryptocurrency, but he agreed with Rhy that it would be nice to narrow the motive down to something manageable. "Did Klem and Irving get subpoenas for the Millers' phone records?"

"They did, but the bank is putting up roadblocks, stating privacy concerns." Rhy shook his head. "Personally, I think they're trying to figure out what Steve Miller was up to prior to his murder. If Miller was doing something illegal, I'd think they'd cooperate."

"Will the feds get involved?" Banks were governed by the Federal Trade Commission, and anything hinky going on within a bank gets attention from the federal government.

"If they find something illegal, yes. But they're not that far into the investigation." Rhy picked up the sticky note. "I'll give Cam a call."

Flynn took that as his cue to leave. He stopped at Gabe's office on the way back to the cubicle. "Do we have the rental?"

"Yep. Just came in." Gabe spoke without turning. "I'm sending you the link and key code to access the place now."

His phone chimed with an incoming message. "Got it. Thanks."

"Anytime." Gabe glanced at him. "Taylor seems nice."

"She is." Flynn managed a smile, although nice was too tame a word to describe Taylor. Beautiful, smart, nurturing, and humble were just some of the traits he admired about her. "She doesn't deserve to be targeted by a killer."

Gabe frowned. "I couldn't agree more. Let me know if you need anything else."

"I will. Thanks." He was about to turn away, then paused. "Actually, I think I should leave the phone here. Taylor's too. Just in case."

"Ah, sure." Gabe opened a desk drawer that was full of snacks. For being lean, Gabe sure liked his snacks. "Power it down and I'll hold on to it for you."

He took a moment to memorize the address and access code, then did as Gabe suggested. Then he hurried out to join Taylor.

"Rhy's going to send someone to my parents' house?" she asked.

"Yes. And we have the rental on Peabody Lake." He held out his hand. "But do me a favor, I'd like you to leave your phone here. We'll pick up new ones along the way."

She nodded and placed her phone in her hand. "I remember doing this last month too."

"Yeah." He tried to smile reassuringly. "I'll leave this in Gabe's office with mine. We can pick them up once this is over."

A moment later, he was back from Gabe's office. Taylor quickly rose to her feet, her expression determined. "I'm ready."

He knew she had little reason to trust him as he escorted her toward the side door of the precinct. He made a mental list in his head. They already had the laptops, but they still needed groceries, disposable phones, and something quick and easy for lunch.

"Is fast food okay for lunch?" He vaguely remembered from their time together last month that she liked salads. "I'm sure I can find a place that offers a variety of salads."

"I'm hungry, so lunch sounds good." She looked tired and worn, and the hour was only half past noon. Her lack of sleep from the night was clearly catching up with her. "But honestly, I could use a thick juicy cheeseburger."

He couldn't help but chuckle. "Sold," he said. "I'm all in."

The next hour passed quickly. He stopped for the phones first, then they hit the grocery store. When that was finished, he picked a drive-through restaurant that boasted single and double cheeseburgers.

The lake house was smaller than it looked online, but the place was clean. There were two bedrooms and a nice living and kitchen area overlooking the lake.

"It's nice," Taylor murmured as they put the groceries away. "Cozy compared to staying at the Millers."

"Are all your clients wealthy?" he asked.

"Most are, yes." She unpacked their cheeseburgers and fries. "I can't lie, they pay me well, and I've been using that money to pay off my student loans."

"You don't have to justify your career choice to me." He joined her at the table.

"Funny, but I seem to remember you thinking my job was easy and brainless," she said.

His jaw dropped. "I never said brainless."

"No, but you can't deny you viewed my job as easy and not very challenging." She arched a brow. "I could read your thoughts clearly on your face."

"I shouldn't have said that." He reached over to take her hand. "Forgive me. The truth was that I didn't trust you back then. Zeke and I were focused on keeping Sienna and Bailey safe. It was never personal."

"I know." She shrugged. "I can understand why you were suspicious of me."

"Because I didn't know you the way I do now." He hesitated, tempted to say more, but then held back. The best way to protect her was to keep their relationship professional. He saw what had happened to Zeke who had fallen for Sienna while he was taking on the role of bodyguard. He couldn't afford to be distracted. Besides, someone as pretty as Taylor wouldn't be interested in him. "I think we should say grace. We have much to be thankful for."

She nodded, then dropped her gaze to her lap. He wasn't used to saying grace, but it was so common a practice with the tactical team that it felt wrong not to give thanks prior to eating a meal.

He cleared his throat. "Dear Lord Jesus, we thank You for this food we are about to eat. We ask that You please keep Taylor's family safe in Your care, and we humbly that You provide the strength and wisdom the police need to bring this ruthless killer to justice. Amen."

"Amen," she echoed.

Was it his imagination, or did her fingers cling to his for a long moment before she released his hand? He glanced over at her, but she appeared to be focused on her meal.

He made quick work of his cheeseburger and fries. Eating fast was common for most cops. Lunch and dinner had to be consumed quickly in case a call came through.

"I guess I should finish going through the mug shots." Taylor's tone lacked enthusiasm. "At least once that's finished, I can move on to something else."

"Yes, I would appreciate that. I'm not sure there's much

else we can do other than wait to hear what the Brookland PD uncovers."

She frowned. "I can't just sit around doing nothing. There must be something else I can do to help find this guy."

He thought about Roman Paulson being shot twice in the chest. "We can try going through social media. But I'm not sure that will help now that Roman is dead. I doubt the killer is on any of the platforms."

"I still can't believe it," she murmured, half to herself. "I didn't know Roman very well, but it's weird to know a member of your family was shot to death."

He couldn't think of anything to say to make her feel better. Maybe Roman had gotten in over his head, gambling debts or something like that, which had led to his involvement in the scheme. Even though he didn't have a lot of experience in doing detective work or running investigations, he kept coming back to the possibility of money laundering.

Organized crime wasn't run by the old Mafia bosses like they were back in his grandfather's day, but the concept still existed. Using computers made the transactions even more impersonal.

When they'd finished eating, he took a moment to power up the disposable phones. Then he called Gabe to give him their new numbers.

"Oh hey, Flynn, Rhy was looking for you. Hang on." Before he could say anything, Gabe put him on hold.

Rhy picked up the call. "I just heard from Cam. He's gone past the Templeton house and found nothing suspicious. However, one of the neighbors called earlier this morning to complain they saw someone peeking into the windows at the home. The guy wore a hoodie, and the hour was such that we don't for sure it was the killer. Cam thinks it was likely kids looking for an easy mark for a robbery."

"Okay, thanks for the update." He gave Taylor a reassuring smile so she wouldn't be alarmed. "Let us know if anything changes. I'm glad Cam is keeping an eye on the place."

"Yep. Stay in touch." Rhy ended the call.

"You've been great through all of this." Taylor rose to clear the table. "I feel guilty for putting you in danger, but I wouldn't be here if not for your expertise."

"I told you my job as a cop is to protect the public." Her gratitude grated on him. "Stop worrying about me."

She tossed their garbage into the container, then swung toward him. She looked exasperated, but he must have read her wrong because she abruptly reached up to pull his head down and kissed him.

CHAPTER SEVEN

Wrong move, Taylor thought seconds before getting swept away in Flynn's kiss. The way he cradled her close sent her heart soaring. But as wonderful as the kiss was, it ended quickly, with Flynn disentangling himself and stepping back. She swallowed a wave of regret for giving in to her impulse to kiss him.

"We, uh, I shouldn't have done that." He looked a bit shell-shocked as he glanced around the small lake house at everything but her. "I need to stay focused."

She was the one who'd kissed him, not the other way around. But he clearly wasn't interested in repeating the experiment. And why was that so depressing? She and Flynn were friends. They wouldn't be together at all if not for the gunman.

"I apologize," she said, owning the situation.

"No need." A flush of embarrassment crept up Flynn's neck. "I, uh, we need to get back to work."

"And that means reviewing mug shots." Once this night-mare was over, she never wanted to see another mug shot ever again.

"Yes." He finally looked at her, his eyes intense. "Finding this guy has to be our top priority."

His dedication was admirable, even if she secretly wished for something more. Something personal. "Okay. I understand."

Flynn looked as if he wanted to say something but didn't. Pushing away from the kitchen counter he crossed to the table and set up the computers. The table was small, and he placed the laptops back-to-back so they were facing each other.

After he'd finished logging into the police database, she sank into the chair and went back to work. She was up to the last names that started with R and found there were many. Once she reached the last six letters of the alphabet, she was sure the process would go by much quicker.

Yet even as she clicked through one photograph after another, she harbored doubts about her ability to find this guy in the system. Either her memory would fail her or he didn't have a criminal record.

Likely both.

Between pictures, she'd look at Flynn working across from her. His red hair was mussed as if he'd run his fingers through it. His square jaw was unshaven, and while he wouldn't be considered handsome in a classical sense, she found him very attractive.

Too attractive.

With a sigh, she tore her gaze away. Flynn couldn't have made it any clearer that he wasn't interested. She needed to accept that they were nothing more than friends while figuring out a way to ignore the awareness between them.

She went through the next photo too fast and had to back up to look at it more closely. The nose on this man's face was large, but after staring at it for a long moment, she decided it didn't match that of the shooter. With a sigh, she kept going.

"Taylor?" She glanced up when Flynn said her name. "Will you take a look at these pictures?"

Curious, she rose and went around the table so she could see his computer screen. She was surprised to find he was logged into social media and had located her cousin Jacob Paulson's page.

"That's Jake, and that's Lyle." She indicated the two men on the screen. The picture was from a few years ago, taken in the summertime where the clear blue water of a lake could be seen behind them. "Where are they?"

"I was hoping you'd recognize it." Flynn waved a hand at the window. "I don't know Peabody Lake well enough to know if this was taken here."

She frowned, trying to recall if anyone in her family had a lake house. "They could be with a friend. Jake and Lyle are only a year apart and could have had similar friends. Roman was two years older than Jake."

"The area doesn't look familiar?" Flynn asked.

"No, but I'm not as familiar with this lake either." She frowned, trying to imagine where the picture may have been taken. "Maybe we should drive around Peabody Lake to see if it was taken here. We might be able to track down that home behind them, on the other side of the lake." The house in question was opulent in appearance, as if it belonged to someone rich or famous.

Like maybe a ball player? Were they wrong about Steve Miller's role of CEO of Brookland Bank being the reason he was murdered? Maybe Robin Miller had stumbled across something while working on her interior design of the Buck's player's house.

"Maybe later," Flynn said.

"Flynn, there are a lot of expensive homes on this lake, on other lakes in the area too," she admitted. "I've heard that some of these homes were purchased by baseball and basketball players. That house behind Jake and Lyle is a multimillion-dollar home. It could be the type of place Robin Miller was hired to redecorate."

Admiration flashed in Flynn's gaze. "Smart thinking. Maybe we should drive around the lake, see if we can find this house."

Even if they did find the home, she wasn't sure what that meant. Her cousins weren't related to any famous athletes that she was aware of. Friends? Maybe, but the date on the picture of her cousins was four years old.

Her initial rush of excitement faded. They could be grasping at straws. Trying to make something out of nothing.

"I should finish going through the mug shots before we do anything else," she said with a sigh. "I don't want to take us off on some sort of wild goose chase, especially if the gunman happens to be in the system. Finding him is the goal, right? We don't know that Roman's brothers are involved in this."

"Right." His expression turned grim. "Better to keep working through the list. In the meantime, I'll keep this photo for future reference."

With a nod, she returned to her chair. Again, she had to force herself to concentrate on the photographs on the screen because her mind wandered back to her cousins. And the conversation she'd had with Robin just days before the brutal murder.

She hated to admit that Flynn may have been right about the need to break off their embrace. She was having enough trouble concentrating on her role in this investigation, and that was without the added emotional baggage that accompanied a relationship.

The next hour passed in silence. As she predicted, there were less names per letter near the end of the alphabet. Then a picture bloomed on the screen that caused her heart to lodge in her throat.

"Flynn?" She couldn't tear her gaze from the computer. "I think I found him."

"Really?" Flynn shot out of his chair, hurrying to stand behind her. "Nickoli Yurgis? Are you sure?"

"The nose is the same." She tapped the screen. "The minute I saw the picture, I remembered it. This guy doesn't have a beard, at least in this photo, but he has dark hair. I can't say with 100 percent accuracy that this man is the shooter, but if it's not him, then it might be another male relative." She glanced up at him over her shoulder. "Can your tech expert, Gabe Melrose, dig into his background?"

"I plan to ask him to do just that." Flynn leaned forward to take control of the computer. He clicked a few keys, then let out a low whistle. "Well, this is interesting. Nickoli Yurgis has ties to the Russian Mafia. And he was arrested three years ago for stabbing a man. Too bad he wasn't convicted, as the only witness to the murder disappeared."

A chill snaked down her spine as she stared at the additional information Flynn had uncovered. Russian Mafia? She hadn't even known such an organization existed. From what she saw on the screen, the alleged stabbing done by this Nickoli Yurgis was as cold-blooded as the murders had been. If this man or someone close to him was the shooter, then the connection to the murders had to be the Brookland Bank and Steve Miller's role as president and CEO.

Detective Klem had mentioned following the money.

A sudden wave of doubt assailed her. What if she was

wrong? What if her memory wasn't as clear as she'd thought?

"Good work, Taylor." Flynn gently squeezed her shoulder, then pulled out his phone. "Gabe? We have a name for you."

She listened as Flynn filled Gabe in on the scant information they'd found included with Nickoli Yurgis's mug shot, hoping and praying she hadn't made a mistake.

That her identification of this man matching her memory of the shooter wasn't sending them the wrong path.

All she could do now was pray.

Please, Lord Jesus, grant us the wisdom we need to find the killer!

EXCITEMENT COURSED through Flynn's veins. Taylor had found the perp, and he had ties to the Russian Mafia! He felt certain they were on the right track, that somehow Steve Miller had gotten mixed up with the wrong people.

"Thanks, Gabe. Please keep me updated on what you find." He lowered the disposable phone, his gaze lingering on the distinctly European features of Nickoli Yurgis.

Figured his last name started with a Y. They should have started going through mug shots from the end of the alphabet.

"Should I keep going?" Taylor asked.

He hesitated, then nodded. "If you don't mind, yes. You're almost finished anyway."

She caught her lower lip between her teeth. "I hope I'm right about him. This looks like the profile I remembered from last night, but it was dark, and I only caught a glimpse as he strode past."

"I trust your instincts," he said gently. "I know the circumstances were dire, and you were scared, but you know what you saw." He cupped her shoulders in his hands. "The fact that you instantly locked on this guy proves that you remember that moment very clearly. I'm proud of you for sticking with it."

"I'm not sure I had much of a choice." She reached up to cover one of his hands with hers. "But thank you. I couldn't have done any of this without you."

He tried to ignore the zip of awareness dancing along his nerves. Their brief yet intense kiss was still too fresh in his mind. It had taken all his willpower, and then some, to pull away. To put distance between them. Physical distance was one thing.

Spending so much time with her was creating an emotional connection that he'd never experienced with anyone else.

Her dropping her hand from his was his cue to do the same. Releasing her, he returned to his computer screen. But his goal of finding more information related to Lyle and Jake Paulson seemed unimportant now that they had a name to go with their suspect.

Then again, Roman Paulson had been murdered, either because he'd gotten involved with the Russian Mafia, too, or like Taylor, because he had seen or heard something he shouldn't have. Resigned, Flynn renewed his efforts to keep searching. Digging through social media was tedious, but Taylor had done her part with going through mug shots, so he would finish this too.

Besides, it was much better to stay busy than to think about kissing her again.

He glanced up at her, marveling at how pretty she was. Logically, he knew she'd only kissed him out of gratitude.

The way she thanked him for keeping her safe grated on his nerves. As if he or any cop would leave an innocent woman in the lurch.

He was nothing special. And it was only a matter of time before she realized that fact for herself.

Twenty minutes later, Taylor rose to her feet and stretched. "I'm finished. There were a surprisingly lot of last names with the letter Z. But Yurgis is the only profile that matches my memory."

"Great job." He flashed a smile. "Relax for a bit. I'll let you know if I come across anything interesting from your cousins."

She frowned. "I really think we should take a drive around the lake. I know it probably won't look the same from the road as it does from the water, but that house is big enough that we should be able to find it without a problem."

He glanced at his watch. It was almost one thirty in the afternoon, but the cloudy sky made it seem darker than usual. Falling back from daylight saving didn't help. The sun would go down earlier than ever. "Too bad we don't have a boat."

"Are you sure about that?" She gestured to the window. "This might be a relatively small house, but most rental properties on a lake include a boat of some sort. And we should do it now before it gets dark."

He considered that for a moment, then nodded. "Good point. Let's check it out."

Taylor pulled on her winter coat as he shrugged into his fleece, zipping it over the gun holster on his hip. The boathouse was down near the shoreline, so he headed out the back door.

The brown grass slopped down to the lake. Taylor's foot slipped on a slick spot, so he caught her hand to steady her.

"Thanks," she murmured. "I don't think early November is a time of the year to take a swim."

The boathouse door had a keypad lock on it, the same make and model as the one on the front door. He punched in the four-digit key code, and the door opened. A musty, stale scent wafted over them.

"No one has been down here in a while," he said. The boathouse was stuffed to the brim. He could barely walk inside, turning sideways to get past the wide-backed Adirondack lawn chairs, two kayaks and paddles, an inner tube, several life vests, and finally what appeared to be a small fishing boat.

"Do you think the motor works?" Taylor's gaze was doubtful as he checked out the fishing boat. While getting to the vessel was difficult from the doorway, he could now see that the boat was positioned up against the single garage door so that it could be easily pushed into the lake.

"If not, we can always use the oars." He wasn't surprised to see two long oars stretched along the bottom of the boat. They were a hint that the motor may not be super reliable.

Or maybe the owners of the lake house just wanted to be sure they provided enough equipment to forestall complaints.

"Are we really doing this?" Taylor asked as he stepped out of the boat and unlatched the garage door. "We're taking the boat out?"

"Yep." He hoisted the garage door open. The lake lapped against the shore, the water higher than usual according to the rocky edge being more than halfway submerged. "We'll be fine as long as it doesn't rain or snow."

Taylor hesitated. "Nobody else is on the lake from what I can see."

He nodded, having noticed that too. The icy chill in the air didn't make for a fun trip across the water, but they wouldn't be out for long. The more he considered their limited options, the more he warmed to the plan. "Don't worry, we'll make it a short trip. Since there isn't anyone else out here, we can do straight down the middle to see if we can spot the house behind your cousins."

"Okay." She placed her hands on her hips, glancing from the boat to the lake with a frown. "I've never been out on a boat before. What do you need me to do?"

He appreciated her willingness to assist. "First, I need to get the boat into the water. Then I'll hold it steady for you to climb in."

Taylor watched as he pulled the small fishing vessel out of the boathouse. She bent over and helped push from her end.

To his surprise, the boat went into the water with relative ease. Clearly the owners and renters had done this before.

"Okay, get in." He held the boat steady with one hand, holding the other out to her. She grasped his hand and gingerly stepped into the boat. It wobbled from side to side, so she quickly sat down on the middle seat.

"Good job." He quickly climbed in behind her, then grabbed one of the long oars. He pressed the flattened edge of the paddle on the grassy shore and leaned on the oar until the boat was floating freely in the water. The small fishing boat motor was tipped up so that the lower blades were out of the way. After sliding the oar back along the bottom of the boat, he moved the motor so that the blades were submerged in the murky water. After two quick pulls on the rope starter, the engine roared to life.

Not bad, he thought. They could probably get from one

end of the lake and back to their rental without a problem. A quick glance at the bottom of the vessel confirmed the boat was sound. He didn't see any sign of water seeping in from a seam or hole. He turned to sit by the engine, steering the boat into the middle of the lake.

"This is nice," Taylor said from her perch on the center seat. "Chilly but nice."

"Once the lake freezes over, you'll see all sorts of ice shanties going up," he said. "Ice fishing is a big deal out here."

She turned to stare at him. "They drill holes in the ice to catch fish?"

"Yep." He smiled when she wrinkled her nose in distaste. "Hey, don't knock it until you try it."

"I like fish, but no thanks on the ice fishing part." She turned back to scan the lakeshore. "You watch that side." She gestured to the aft side of the boat. "I'll watch this one."

The putt-putt of the motor seemed loud in the stillness of the day. Most adults were working while the kids were still in school.

The wind cut through his fleece, making him wish he had a puffy winter coat like Taylor's. Doing his best to ignore the cold, he scanned the homes lining the shore. Most were huge and expensive, but every once in a while, there was a smaller home, much like the one they were currently renting.

Not everyone living out here was rich and famous.

They were almost all the way across the lake when Taylor waved her arm. "There! That's the house!"

She was right, there was no mistaking the three-story structure that loomed large on the aft side of the lake. Since that house had been behind her cousins in the photo, he turned to look at the property across from it. This section of

Peabody Lake was narrower, so it was easy to see both properties.

The house directly across was enormous as well, and the boathouse sported an open deck that was clearly used for entertaining. Thinking back to the picture, he believed the Paulson brothers had been standing up on that deck when the photo was taken.

Making a mental note of the location of the home, he turned the boat engine, making a wide turn to head back to the rental property. Back in early June, when Grayson had been trying to track a killer on this very lake, Gabe had managed to identify the owner of a property that helped crack the case wide open.

Maybe their tech guru could do the same thing again now.

Even as the thought formed, he had to admit there was no indication that Taylor's cousins were involved. Or that the lake house where they'd taken a picture would lead to a connection with the Russian Mafia.

Asking Gabe to track down the homeowners could be a waste of time. Digging into Nickoli Yurgis was more important. They really needed to find him or any of his known associates. If not? They would be right back where they'd started.

Having a name didn't mean much if the guy was hiding deep underground.

Feeling grim, he cast his gaze over the lake. A hint of movement caught his eye, giving him pause.

Someone else was out on the lake too.

The tiny hairs on the back of his neck lifted in alarm. He instinctively angled closer to the shoreline on the same side of the lake as their rental house.

"Taylor? I need you to crouch down in the boat." He strove to keep his voice steady.

"Why?" Then she saw it too. Without hesitation, she slid from the center bench until she was sitting on the bottom of the boat. Ducking her head, she asked, "Can you see who is in the other boat?"

"Not yet." He didn't like the fact that the boat was coming straight for them. The engine of the second vessel grew louder and louder as the boat closed the gap. And he felt certain it was bigger than the fishing boat engine putt-putting beneath his fingers.

He gave the boat as much gas as he could, but their speed didn't change. Swallowing hard, he knew they weren't going to make it back to the rental. The fishing boat was no match for the big powerful boat coming toward them.

"Lord Jesus, save us!"

Hearing Taylor's desperate prayer gave him an idea. He abruptly yanked on the handle of the engine, bringing the boat in a tight turn. One thing about having a smaller vessel was that it was more agile.

Then he deliberately cut across the path of the oncoming boat like crossing the letter *T*.

In response, the driver tried to turn as well. But he was going too fast, and the boat was too big to respond quickly.

Swerving around the back of the boat, Flynn tried desperately to get back to the rental house. Then he heard the boat coming up behind them.

He made another quick turn to face the threat. He pulled his weapon from beneath the fleece as the crack of gunfire rang out. Seeing the gun in the boat driver's hand pointed at them, he didn't hesitate to return fire. Unfortunately, holding one hand on the boat's tiller and moving across the water while firing meant he didn't hit the perp.

Hearing several metallic pings, he belatedly realized the driver of the boat was drilling their fishing boat with bullets, likely because it was easier to hit the boat than a person. Water was already seeping in from the various bullet holes.

"Flynn?" Taylor's voice was fearful. "What can we do?"

"Stay down." He shifted to copy the perp's idea, aiming at his much larger boat. The driver abruptly turned the vessel and sped away in the opposite direction.

There was nothing he could do to stop the gunman from getting away. As icy water sloshed over his shoes, he understood they didn't have a second to waste.

"Come on, come on," he whispered as he headed toward their rental house. If they sank much farther, they'd risk being submerged in the lake and succumbing to hypothermia.

The fishing boat engine abruptly died. Abandoning the tiller, he grabbed the oars, which were completely covered in murky lake water.

They were still twenty yards from shore, but he set the oars in the small holes on either side of the boat and pulled with all his might. They had to get back to solid ground.

They just had to!

Taylor had found a small bucket and was desperately trying to get the water out of the boat. It was a losing battle. He abruptly stopped rowing and reached for her. "We need to swim the rest of the way."

"Swim?" Her voice was little more than a croak, and he realized she was already shivering. Hypothermia was already setting in.

If they didn't get out of the lake very soon, they would die.

CHAPTER EIGHT

Icy water filled the boat faster than she could bail. Taylor's lower limbs went numb first, then she noticed her arms weren't working properly. The water was almost up to her waist now, and the boat was sinking fast.

They were going to die.

"Swim!" Flynn's shout managed to penetrate the icy numbness enveloping her. He tugged her along with him as they quickly abandoned the boat. "Swim!"

Desperation spurred her forward. Looking beyond Flynn's shoulder, she could see the shoreline wasn't far. Maybe twenty yards? Yet it seemed unattainable.

Forcing her dead limbs to move wasn't easy. She tried to kick her legs to propel her forward. But she couldn't feel them moving. Flynn had a tight grip on her jacket and was pulling her along.

"Stand up." He abruptly surged from the water, taking a few stumbling steps. "The shore is right there! Come on, Taylor, you can do this!"

Understanding the water wasn't very deep here, she struggled to stand. Her legs didn't want to support her, but she managed to take two steps before falling back down.

"Hang on to me." Flynn anchored his arm around her waist and hauled her forward. He must be just as cold as she was, but he had sheer strength of will on his side. He pulled her up and out of the water, collapsing on the shore.

"Wh-where are we?" The area didn't look familiar.

"The lake house is the next one over." Flynn pushed himself upright. "We need to move. I don't know if he'll come back."

The idea of the gunman tracking them down and firing more shots sent the fight-or-flight response jolting through her. She was still cold to the bone, but she forced herself to lift up onto her hands and knees. With Flynn's help, she managed to lever herself upright.

"This way." Flynn guided her across the lawn at an angle. The house appeared to be empty, or maybe she just assumed that as no one rushed out to help them.

Once they were in the yard of their rental property, the trek became more difficult. Not only were her legs not working well, but they were climbing up the slope to the house. It felt like scaling Everest, her gaze focused on the warmth of the building so close yet so far away.

"You can do it," Flynn said between grunts. "We're almost there."

He was doing more than his part, hauling her along with him. When they reached the house, he punched in the key code and opened the door. The blast of warm air was like a blanket. She wanted to lie down on the floor, but Flynn wouldn't let her.

"No, Taylor. We need to keep moving." He urged her forward. "We need to take off our wet clothes and grab some blankets for the road."

For the road? She blinked. Stared. "We're leaving?"

"Yes. As quickly as possible." He dragged her to the closest bedroom and wrenched the quilted blanket off the bed. "Strip off your wet clothes and wrap up in this."

Strip?

"If you can't take your things off, I'll do it for you." Flynn was already shucking off his wet clothes. She belatedly realized he'd grabbed another blanket from the closet.

"I can do it." Or so she hoped. The numbness was wearing off, leaving a strange tingling along her nerve endings. She began to shiver uncontrollably as she peeled off her coat and her sweater.

"Here, let me help." Flynn draped the quilt around her shoulders. The warmth was amazing, giving her the strength she needed to toe off her shoes and begin to peel down her wet jeans.

The only thought in her mind was survival. The gunman had tried to drown them in the icy water. Flynn was right to get them out of there.

"Good job," he said as she managed to kick the jeans off. He drew the edges of the quilt around her and looked into her eyes. "The worst is over. We're going to get through this. Time to head out to the car."

She nodded, ignoring the absurdity of driving away wearing nothing but wet underwear and a blanket. "Okay."

With a reassuring smile, he drew her down the short hall to the main living area. She belatedly realized that he'd tucked his blanket under his arms so that he could hold his service weapon in one hand, carrying his wallet with the other as they made their way through the house.

He ignored the computers, grabbing the car's key fob off the counter. He opened the garage door and peeked through, then moved into the garage.

She quickly snagged one of the laptops, yanking the power cord from the wall to follow him. *It is better than nothing,* she thought, as she wrestled with keeping the quilt around her as she headed to the passenger side of the vehicle.

This time, Flynn opened the garage door, taking another moment to peer outside before sliding in behind the wheel. They probably looked ridiculous, two people practically naked wrapped in blankets sitting in the front seat of the SUV.

All that mattered was that they'd survived.

"Thank you, Lord Jesus," she whispered.

"Amen." Flynn looked both ways before taking a left at the end of the driveway. They'd come in from the opposite direction, but she didn't question his decision.

Flynn had saved her life. If not for his dragging her through the water and half carrying her up the embankment, she wouldn't be sitting beside him. She'd never felt God's presence the way she did now.

She knew God had given Flynn the strength he needed to get them out of there.

Amen, she silently added.

Flynn was silent as he drove. They didn't have anything but the blankets, the computer, and the SUV. Neither one of them was even wearing shoes. Flynn cranked the heat, which felt good on her bare toes. Their new disposable cell phones had been rendered useless after being submerged in the lake water. The only saving grace was that Flynn had his wallet and his gun.

"What should we do?" she asked as they continued their meandering drive. "We can't call anyone for help."

"I know." He glanced at the computer she'd tucked on the floor at her feet. "Smart of you to grab the laptop.

Once we're settled, we'll use that to reach out to the team."

"Settled where?" She shivered again, despite the warm air blasting through the vents. Their near miss was still difficult to comprehend. She was having trouble keeping herself from thinking about how close they'd come to dying.

"The American Lodge," Flynn said. "I planned to avoid it, but we don't have many options. I know the owner, Gary Campbell. He's a former firefighter and offers discounts to all police and firefighters. Our team has worked with him often in the past two years. I know he'll give us connecting rooms without a problem." Flynn shot her a wry look. "My wallet is soaked, but I'm confident he'll take cash, even if it's wet and needs to dry off."

She'd never heard of the American Lodge but trusted Flynn's instincts. Especially since it seemed as if he knew this Gary on a first-name basis.

"I'm surprised you didn't think to head there rather than renting the house on Peabody Lake."

"I discussed that with Cassidy." He grimaced. "It's located in Brookland, so I immediately took it off the list. I also wanted to avoid going anyplace that had ties to the tactical team. But without a phone, that's the only place that will work. I'm concerned that even with using Gabe Melrose to secure the lake house, the gunman found us."

She frowned, thinking back on those frightening moments on the lake. "I hadn't considered the possibility we were followed to the lake. I assumed the perp was in one of the houses and saw us going by. How else did he get a boat to come after us?"

Flynn shot her a quick glance. "That's a good point. Most people pull their boats out of the water in the winter." He scowled and shook his head. "I don't know what to think. Did we really rent a house on the same lake where the mastermind behind the murders lives?"

She swallowed hard. "Maybe. A professional hit man wouldn't own a house on Peabody Lake, but the person who hired him could have a residence there. That meshes with the photo we found of Lyle and Jake Paulson. And that would explain how he'd happened to see us on the lake and had access to a boat to chase after us."

"Yeah, that's the only scenario that makes sense to me," Flynn said. He raked a hand through his wet hair. "We really need to talk to Rhy, and soon."

She nodded. Glancing down at the quilt wrapped around her, she was conscious of her wet undergarments. The feeling had returned to her body, but she still felt chilled. She was tempted to ask about how soon they could get replacement clothes and shoes but understood Flynn's priority was to get them safely to the American Lodge.

Everything else was secondary.

They had survived this round, but what about the next attempt? As Flynn continued taking back roads to get out of the city of Peabody, she couldn't help but pray that the Brookland PD would find and arrest the gunman.

Very soon.

WAVES OF GUILT washed over Flynn as he took every back road he could find to get far away from Peabody. This mess was his fault.

He'd nearly gotten them killed. His bright idea of heading out onto the lake to see if they could find the location of the homes in the picture of the Paulson brothers had backfired in a big way.

The events had unfolded so quickly he still wasn't sure how they'd gotten out of the lake. His only clear memory was grabbing and holding on to Taylor. One minute they were taking gunfire, the next they were stumbling onto the lake shore. How he'd managed to keep ahold of both Taylor and his weapon was another mystery.

The only answer was that God had guided and protected them.

And while he was grateful for that, he needed to be smarter moving forward. Swallowing hard against the bitter taste of failure, he forced himself to think logically. They had no clothes and no phones. He had his credit cards, but he didn't want to use them.

Was it smart to seek refuge at the American Lodge? He honestly didn't know.

Another temporary location? He didn't necessarily want to drive to any of his teammate's homes. For one thing, he wasn't sure they'd be there. But more importantly, he wasn't willing to bring danger to their doorsteps.

Rhy lived in Brookland with his pregnant wife and one-year-old daughter. Flynn would never bring danger to the Finnegan homestead, but using the American Lodge even as a temporary staging area would make it more convenient for Rhy or any of the others to come to them.

They needed clothes, shoes, replacement phones, more cash, and time to regroup. Not necessarily in that order.

Tightening his grip on the steering wheel, he held his emotions in check as he backtracked twice to make sure they weren't being followed. By the time they reached the American Lodge, a white two-story motel with twelve rooms on each level, every one of his nerves was stretched to a breaking point.

Was he making another mistake by coming here?

Second-guessing every move he made wasn't helpful. Flynn couldn't afford to be paralyzed by overthinking their next steps. Yet he didn't trust himself not to screw up again either.

"This looks nice," Taylor said.

He managed a nod, reaching over to place his service weapon in the glove box. "I'd like you to stay here while I get our rooms. It shouldn't take long."

"Okay." Her smile didn't quite reach her eyes.

Keenly aware of his state of undress, he slid out from behind the wheel, taking a moment to secure the blanket around his torso. Then he grabbed his wallet. On his way to the lobby, he glanced around, hoping no one would notice. A man wearing nothing but a blanket would be easy to remember. Thankfully, there weren't too many cars in the parking lot, giving him hope that Gary would be able to accommodate his request.

Gary was sitting behind the desk when he entered the lobby. The older man's eyebrows hiked up upon seeing Flynn.

"What in the world happened?" Gary asked. "Looks like you've been swimming."

"Yeah, you could say that." He was relieved Gary had taken his bedraggled appearance in stride. "I need a couple of connecting rooms."

"Of course, rooms 11 and 12 are open on the first floor." Gary frowned as he set his water-soaked wallet on the counter. "No need to pay now, I can understand if you need to dry out first."

"Thanks, but I don't know how long we'll be staying." He unfolded the wallet and drew out several wet bills. "Sorry about them being wet."

"Money is money," Gary said with a shrug. He took

the wet bills, set them out flat to dry, then slid two key cards toward him. "Is there something else I can do for you?"

It was comforting to know Gary was an ally, a friend when he desperately needed one. "Just keep an eye on the security cameras while I make some calls."

"Yeah, sure." Gary nodded solemnly. "Take care of yourself, Flynn."

"Thanks." He turned away, paused, then glanced back at Gary. "Did you know Steve and Robin Miller?"

Gary considered that for a moment. "Are you talking about the same Steve Miller who is the president of Brookland Bank?"

"Yeah. Exactly."

"I didn't know him personally," Gary said. "But I have my business account with Brookland Bank. Why? Did something happen?"

He shouldn't have been surprised that Gary used the local bank for his business. Yet hearing him say the words were still a shock. "Steve and Robin were murdered last night. I'd appreciate it if you would keep our being here under wraps."

"I always do." Gary frowned. "Murdered? I must have missed that on the news."

"Yeah, well, I'm not sure how much information the police are telling the public about the incident." Flynn held Gary's gaze. "Please don't say anything about us being here."

"Us who?" Gary waved a hand, looking impatient. "You should know me better than that. Your secret is safe with me."

Flynn nodded his thanks, turned, and pushed through the door. He told himself to stop being paranoid. Gary

Campbell had been a friend of the Finnegans, their cousins the Callahans, and the entire tactical team.

Gary would never betray them. Just because he did his banking at the same place where the CEO was killed didn't mean anything.

He slid in behind the wheel, set the wallet and key cards in the cupholder, then drove around to the far corner of the building. The connecting rooms were familiar as many other members of the team had used them in the past. The pair of rooms were located near the staircase leading to the second floor. Out of habit, he parked the vehicle out of sight from the parking lot.

"Stay behind me," Flynn advised as he and Taylor got out of the SUV. The ground was cold beneath his bare feet, and he never realized how important shoes were until this moment. If they had to go on the run, they'd be sunk.

He tried to keep a positive attitude as he unlocked the door to room 12, then handed Taylor the key card. "Open your side of the connecting door between the rooms, okay?" She'd brought the laptop computer with her, which made him remember he needed to grab his gun.

Five minutes later, he was using the motel desk phone to call Rhy. Unfortunately, his boss didn't answer. He left a terse message. "Rhy, we're at the American Lodge and need clothes, shoes, phones, and cash. Please call ASAP, thanks."

Taylor sank down onto the edge of the bed, drawing the edge of the quilt up and over her shoulder. "How long before he calls back?"

"I'm sure it will be soon." He forced a smile as he crossed to the thermostat and cranked the heat. "Try to relax for a few minutes. We're safe here."

Even as he said the words, he squelched another flash of guilt. Hadn't he said that while at the lake house?

For the first time since this nightmare started, he seriously considered handing Taylor's safety over to another member of the team. Maybe he wasn't qualified to protect her. He'd done his best to stay focused on the case, but he'd failed miserably.

This was part of the reason he'd broken off from their kiss.

He couldn't afford to be distracted.

"This isn't your fault, Flynn." As if reading his mind, Taylor crossed to his side. "I can see you mentally beating yourself up over what happened. Remember, it was my idea to see if we could find the house in the lake photograph featuring my cousins."

Had she? He shook his head. "I'm the one who put us in harm's way."

"You're the one who saved my life." Clutching the ends of the quilt in one hand, she placed the other on his arm. "I wouldn't have made it out of there without you."

That didn't make him feel any better since she'd only been in the lake because of his harebrained plan. But the hotel phone rang, preventing him from saying anything more.

"That's Rhy." He brushed past her to grab the phone. "Yeah?"

"What on earth happened?" Rhy asked, concern lacing his tone. "You need me to bring clothes and shoes?"

"Yes." He dropped to the edge of the bed. "It's a long story. Bottom line, we're safe but need help."

"Of course," Rhy said without hesitation. "Give me your sizes and I'll grab new stuff for you both."

Flynn gestured for Taylor to join him. After giving out the requested information, he said, "Thanks, Rhy. I appreciate your support more than you know."

"I'll be there soon. And Flynn? Stop beating yourself up. Every one of us has been in difficult situations, barely managing to escape unscathed. We are humans who do not have the ability to foresee the future. Take comfort in knowing God has been watching over you and is always there for you. I'll be there in thirty or less." Without saying anything more, Rhy ended the call.

Rhy's words were a balm to his soul. If he thought about some of the situations his teammates had been in, they'd made mistakes too. His boss was right about the fact that no one could see the future. Except God.

The only reason to look backward was to learn from his mistakes.

They just needed a better plan moving forward.

"It's wonderful you have Rhy to depend on," Taylor said, breaking the silence.

"Yes. I am blessed to work with an amazing team." He turned to face her. "And we will all do our best to keep you safe."

"I know." Her smile seemed a bit sad. "I just wish there was more we could do to find the gunman."

"We'll find him." He spoke with confidence, despite wearing a blanket in lieu of clothes. "He made one mistake today; he'll make others."

She looked thoughtful. "Do you have any idea how many people live on Peabody Lake?"

Too many, he thought with a sigh, then he reached for the phone. He'd call Gabe and have him run a list of property owners on the lake. If he remembered correctly, they had run a similar list back when Grayson had a run-in with a gunman on Peabody Lake back in June.

"Hello?" Gabe's voice was hesitant, likely because he didn't recognize the number.

"It's Flynn. We're at the American Lodge."

"Wait, what happened at the lake house?" Gabe asked.

Thinking about how the boat sank made him wince. So much for staying under budget. He quickly filled Gabe in on what had transpired. "I'm sorry, but we'll have to pay for a new boat and new blankets."

"I'm just glad you're okay," Gabe said. "I feel bad that using my name to rent the place didn't protect you."

"It's not your fault; in fact, that's why I'm calling. I need a list of all Peabody Lake property owners. I know you ran one a while back for Grayson, but I could use an updated listing."

"That's easy enough," Gabe said. "Do you want me to email it to you?"

"Yes. Taylor was smart enough to grab one of the laptops as we ran out of there." He flashed her a smile. "Rhy's on his way with clothes and other necessities for us."

"I'll send it over as soon as I have it," Gabe promised. "And really, Flynn, I'm glad you're okay."

"We've been blessed," he said lightly. "Oh, and Rhy will be getting another set of phones for us, so keep answering calls from unknown numbers."

Gabe chuckled. "Considering what's been happening over the past few years, I always do."

"I'll be in touch." He lowered the handset into the cradle. "We'll look at the property list together once Gabe has it," he said to Taylor. "I'll want to know if you recognize any of the names."

"Happy to help." She frowned, then added, "I keep thinking about that picture of Lyle and Jake Paulson. We never did figure out the address of that house."

"Not yet, but when we get the list from Gabe, we'll run a search. I'm sure we'll be able to narrow it down." The idea of gaining key information after their recent colossal failure was encouraging. That and knowing that he was never alone when it came to Taylor's safety provided an acute sense of relief. "Don't worry, we'll get to the bottom of this."

"I know." She reached out to take his hand, but the quilt slid down causing her to quickly grab it. "I never realized how vulnerable it feels to be without clothes."

"No lie." He still had trouble realizing they'd escaped the lake house with just blankets for cover. "This is a first for me too."

A hint of awareness shimmered between them. It had nothing to do with wearing blankets instead of clothes, but that they'd barely survived hypothermia.

Remembering his need to stay focused, he abruptly shot to his feet. Hitching the blanket up, he crossed to the computer. Maybe he could do some searches of his own until Rhy arrived.

Taylor came over to sit beside him. He turned on the computer and was in the process of logging into his email provider when the motel landline phone rang. He almost tripped over the end of the blanket in his haste to answer. "Hello?"

"Flynn, it's Rhy. I'll be there in ten minutes or less."

"Okay, we're currently sitting in room 11." He peered through the opening between the curtains covering the window overlooking the parking lot. "We'll watch for you."

"Great. I have some news from Detective Klem," Rhy said, his tone somber.

His gut clenched. Now what? He tried not to show his dismay. "Anything useful about the case?"

"Not exactly. He and Iverson went to the apartment shared by Lyle and Jake Paulson. They didn't find either man or evidence that they were harmed, but the place was trashed. Like completely searched as if someone was looking for something important."

Flynn sank back down onto the edge of the bed. "Like what?"

"I don't know," Rhy said. "But it adds a new dimension to the case."

That was putting it mildly. A professional hit man murders three people, Steve and Robin Miller and Taylor's cousin Roman Paulson. Now suddenly the killer is searching for something in Lyle and Jake's apartment?

It didn't make any sense. The new puzzle piece didn't fit at all. And he feared they'd never learn the truth in time to prevent another attack against Taylor.

CHAPTER NINE

Clutching the edges of the quilt close, Taylor eyed Flynn's grim expression. Whatever news he'd been given wasn't good.

Another murder? She prayed that wasn't the case.

"See you soon." Flynn dropped the receiver in the cradle, then raked a hand through his hair, making the ends stick up as they had yet to shower after their swim in Peabody Lake. "Rhy will be here in about ten minutes."

"What happened?" When he didn't immediately respond, she narrowed her gaze. "Don't keep me in the dark, Flynn. I'm in danger, and I want to know what's going on."

He sighed, then nodded. "The Brookland detectives went to the apartment shared by your cousins Lyle and Jake Paulson. There's no sign of them or blood indicating they've been hurt," he swiftly added. "But the place has been trashed. Like searching for something and getting angry when you didn't find it trashed."

She frowned. "I don't understand. Why would a professional hit man do that?"

"Yeah, exactly the point. It's not typical behavior for a

man committing a triple homicide. It adds a wrinkle to the case."

"But there's no sign my cousins were killed?" she asked.

"So far the police are operating under the assumption they're alive." He hesitated, then added, "But the destruction of the apartment isn't a good sign. It seems to indicate your cousins are involved with whatever is going on."

"I understand." She wasn't sure how to feel about that. She wasn't close to her Paulson cousins, but they had played together as kids. It was difficult to comprehend how the youngsters she remembered had turned into criminals.

Because clearly they've gotten themselves involved in something dangerous. And Roman had already been brutally murdered as a result. "Maybe identifying the property owners on Peabody Lake will help point us in the right direction." A sudden thought occurred to her. "Maybe Lyle and Jake are at that house now."

"I had considered that, but if the gunman who found us on the lake and drilled bullets into the boat is the same one who trashed their house, then that's not likely."

"You're right." Her shoulders slumped. "I guess I was just looking for a reason to believe they're still alive."

"Don't dwell on the worst-case scenario," he said calmly. "Better to focus on trying to figure out who the gunman is and why he has killed so many people."

"We know who he is, Nickoli Yurgis." She still had trouble believing the gunman had ties to the Russian Mafia. "But why he was hired to kill the Millers is a mystery. I highly doubt he owns any of the property on Peabody Lake."

"True." Flynn rose and crossed the room to peer out the window, then turned to face her. "Have faith we'll find him."

She managed a smile, pulling the edge of the quilt up over her shoulder. Rhy couldn't get there with replacement clothes soon enough. "I will do my best."

"Me too." Flynn held her gaze for a long moment, then glanced through the window again. "I think that's Rhy now."

She turned to look out the window in time to see a black SUV roll slowly through the parking lot. Seeing it reminded her of how the third black SUV she'd noticed while they'd been at Zeke's place. "How do you know it's Rhy and not the gunman?"

Flynn shot her a quick glance. "I recognize Rhy's blond hair and his license plate. Don't worry, we're safe here for now."

For now was the part that worried her, but she didn't say anything. It didn't take long for Rhy to get out of the SUV and grab what seemed to be a huge bag of clothing from the back seat.

Flynn opened the door. "Thanks for getting here so quickly."

"You have Devon to thank for that; she helped make quick work of our little shopping expedition." Rhy gave her a quick nod. "My wife was determined to make sure you had everything you needed."

"That's very sweet." Taylor was touched by how Rhy's wife had chipped in to buy her clothing. She had tried hard not to imagine Rhy buying her underwear. "Make sure you let her know how grateful I am for everything she's done."

"I will." Rhy dropped the bag on the bed. "I'm pretty sure I have everything you need, including basic toiletries. And a pair of disposable phones." Rhy glanced at the computer. "I'm glad you were able to salvage one of the laptops."

"That was Taylor's idea," Flynn was quick to give her credit, as if she'd done something impressive, which she hadn't. Flynn gestured to the two of them. "As you can tell by the blankets, we couldn't take much with us."

"Smart thinking to focus on getting out of there." Rhy stepped back to give them room to access the contents of the bag. "You should both grab clean clothes, shower, and change. We'll talk about next steps once you're finished."

Just thinking about a hot shower had her rummaging in the bag. She quickly found the clothes, undergarments, and shoes Devon had picked out for her. Gathering them close, she made her way through the connecting door to her room.

Thirty minutes later, she emerged from the bathroom feeling completely refreshed. Everything fit better than she could have hoped, from the soft denim jeans to the dark-blue fleece, and the best of all, thick socks and running shoes. The toiletries Devon had chosen were great too. She hadn't realized how awful her hair had smelled until she'd gotten a whiff of the shampoo and conditioner.

Being able to use a blow-dryer was a bonus. With dry hair, she felt warm for the first time in what seemed like eons but was only an hour or two.

Hearing the rumble of deep male voices, she pushed the door of their connecting rooms open. Both men instantly turned to look at her.

"Have a seat." Flynn jumped to his feet. He was freshly showered and shaved and looked amazing. She hadn't appreciated his good looks and strength when she'd met him back in October, but now she was acutely aware of him on every level. Most importantly, his consideration and thoughtfulness. "I'm making coffee if you're interested."

"That would be wonderful, thanks." She took his chair

near the small table and glanced between the two men. "What did I miss?"

"Nothing important," Flynn hastened to assure her. "I filled Rhy in on the details regarding our incident on Peabody Lake. We've discussed the most likely scenario is that the man who hired the gunman to shoot the Millers lives there. Likely in the same house where the photograph was taken of your cousins Lyle and Jake."

She nodded, having come to the same conclusion. "But then something happened that turned the owner of the house against the Millers and my cousins."

"Yes." Flynn crossed to the coffee maker. "And I still think that whatever they were doing somehow involves the bank."

"Detectives Klem and Irving are interviewing the bank staff, but so far they have not come up with anything significant," Rhy said, picking up the thread of their conversation. "The feds have also gotten involved, determined to make sure nothing illegal was going on with the bank's financial statements."

Flynn handed her a cup of coffee with creamer and sugar. Just the way she liked it. She cradled the cup between her hands. "I'm glad the feds are involved. Will that speed up the investigation?"

"I'm not sure." Flynn glanced at Rhy, and added, "Brady Finnegan works for the FBI, but not necessarily in the finance division. Rhy wants to update his brother on the possible link to Peabody Lake."

"Brady will keep us in the loop," Rhy said. "He's not as territorial as other feds."

"I'm all for getting help from as many resources as possible," she said. "Especially if that means Nickoli Yurgis is found and arrested sooner than later."

"Great. I'll contact Brady." Rhy rose and moved to a corner of the room to make the call.

Sipping her coffee, she eyed Flynn. "How long do you think we can stay here?"

He had filled his coffee cup, too, and sat on the edge of the bed across from her. "Rhy and I have been debating that. He thinks we'll be fine here for the next twenty-four hours." He shrugged. "I'm not sure what to do. I've requested access to the safe house, but it's currently in use. Rhy has put us on the list."

That there was a list of people waiting to use a safe house was disconcerting. Not that she should be surprised by the criminal activity necessitating such a thing. Yet her role as a live-in nanny had isolated her from the harsher side of life.

Until now.

The brutal murders of Steve and Robin Miller changed everything. She sipped her coffee, doing her best to stay positive now that the feds were involved in the case. If the federal government couldn't solve this thing, then she wasn't sure who could. In all honesty, she had more faith in the feds working with Flynn, Rhy, and the other members of the team over the Brookland PD.

Still, it was difficult to sit back and do nothing while waiting for Nickoli Yurgis to be arrested.

Glancing at Flynn, she wondered how long he'd stick by her. How long it would be until he handed her over to someone else to deal with?

The thought filled her with dread. Maybe her attachment to Flynn Ryerson wasn't healthy, but she didn't care.

He was the only one she truly trusted.

THE MOMENT RHY had mentioned contacting his brother Brady, Flynn had felt a sick sense of dread. Not that he didn't trust Brady, or the other federal agents their team had worked with over the past few years. He didn't like having more law enforcement officials involved.

Despite his early thought of handing Taylor over to someone else to watch over, his gut rejected that idea now. He couldn't explain the rationale, but he didn't want to walk away from Taylor. Not even if that meant she would stay in a safe house with the feds watching over her.

It didn't make any sense for him to feel this way. After all, he'd nearly gotten them both killed out on Peabody Lake.

Still, there was so much about this case that was unknown. Back in July he'd helped Roscoe keep his pregnant fiancée, Libby, safe from the drug cartel. In the process, they'd uncovered a dirty DEA agent, a fact that had almost caused Roscoe and federal agent Doug Bridges to be killed.

In the big scheme of things, Flynn knew it was rare to run across law enforcement officials on the take. But knowing that didn't shake the irrational fear that he should not leave Taylor alone with anyone else.

"Okay, Brady is going to talk to the agents in charge of the Miller homicide investigation," Rhy said, interrupting his thoughts. "He'll be in touch when he knows something more, but he is fairly certain the agents will want to talk to Taylor in person."

"No way." The refusal burst out before he could think about it. At Rhy's arched brow, he quickly added, "I mean there's no reason to put her in danger. She doesn't know anything about Steve Miller's bank practices."

"I understand what you're saying, but I'm not sure we'll

be able to keep them from talking to Taylor." Rhy spread his hands. "The FBI offices should be safe enough."

"It's not like gunmen haven't targeted both our precinct and the federal office building before." He strove to keep his tone level. "I don't like it."

"We'll work with Brady and Doug to protect Taylor," Rhy said.

There was a long silence as he and Rhy eyed each other warily.

"I'm right here," Taylor finally said. "You're talking about me as if I don't have a say in this matter."

Hiding a wince, he turned to her. "You are a part of this, but I'm just trying to keep you safe."

"From the feds?" she asked in exasperation. "Come on, Flynn. I doubt they're involved in anything illegal."

"And you're willing to bet your life on that?"

"Come on, Flynn," Rhy said. "We're more than capable of keeping her safe."

Outnumbered, he suppressed a sigh. "Fine, but that means you and I go with her to the FBI office building. If you can't come, I'm happy to have someone else from the team accompany us. Once we arrive, we'll wait for Brady to come out to the SUV and escort us into the building."

Rhy nodded. "Okay, that works. But you're right in that I can't be the one to ride shotgun. I have a meeting with Assistant Chief Michaels this afternoon. I'll send Cassidy in my place if that's okay."

"Fine with me." He would have been happier to avoid the meeting all together, but if that wasn't an option, then the extra precautions would have to do.

"And I'm in agreement too," Taylor said. "Not that anyone has asked my opinion."

He turned toward her. "Your opinion matters, but we are the experts when it comes to staying safe."

She grimaced. "I understand that and trust your judgment, Flynn. But I don't appreciate being talked about as if I'm not a part of this. As if I didn't hear the murders and see the gunman walking by."

He was about to apologize when Rhy spoke. "By the way, Gabe has been trying to look into the gunman, Nickoli Yurgis, but so far there's hardly anything online about the guy. The only tidbit Gabe uncovered was that Yurgis had supposedly returned to Serbia, his place of birth, after being released from jail."

"He's not in Serbia now," Taylor said with a frown. "I know I saw him last night at the Millers."

"I believe you and so do the feds," Rhy said reassuringly. "But that's the other reason I needed to get Brady involved. Yurgis adds an international aspect to the homicide investigation. Only the FBI has the resources to coordinate with law enforcement officials within foreign countries to get information on the guy."

Flynn could only imagine how Detectives Klem and Irving felt about having the feds swoop in to take over their case. They wouldn't like it any better than he did. Yet everything Rhy said was true. They needed resources to get to the bottom of this mess.

Which meant there was no way to get around the upcoming interview.

As if on cue, Rhy's phone chirped. His boss glanced at the screen, then said, "Brady says the feds would like to speak to Taylor at four o'clock this afternoon."

Flynn glanced at his watch. "That only gives us an hour."

"I understand, but it's better to get this done and over with," Rhy said.

"Fine. Go ahead and tell Brady we'll be there at four."

"Done." Rhy moved toward the door. "I'll send Cass over too. You know where the FBI office building is in Ravenswood, right?"

"Yeah." The building itself was nothing special, at least from the outside. He followed his boss to the door. "Thanks for everything, Rhy."

"Don't forget to give my thanks to Devon too," Taylor called.

"Will do." Rhy smiled, then headed out to his SUV.

Flynn locked the door behind him, then turned to Taylor. "While we wait for Cassidy to arrive, I plan to review the list of property owners from Gabe. I think the email popped up while we were talking."

Her eyes widened with interest. "I'd like that. I feel like knowing who hired Nickoli will help put an end to the danger."

He wasn't as convinced but quickly took control of the keyboard. He would have preferred to print the list out on paper, but he didn't want to head inside to Gary's small business office to do that. Pulling up the list, he made the print large enough that they could both see the names without squinting.

"Let me know if any of the names looks familiar," he said as he began to scan them.

"Okay." Taylor leaned so close he could smell the citrusy scent of her shampoo.

For long moments, there was nothing but silence as they went through the names. Flynn wasn't sure what he'd expected, but none of the names leaped out at him.

Taylor leaned back in her chair. "None of the names on the first page ring a bell for me."

He was impressed she'd gotten through the names so quickly. "You read faster than I do, so give me a minute to finish up."

She grinned. "Reading is my superpower," she joked.

After finishing the names on the first page, he moved on to the second. But much like the first page, none of the property owners' names jumped out at him.

"What about this one?" Taylor asked, tapping the screen. "Investments, Inc."

He hadn't gotten that far, but as he scanned the page, he saw it. Gabe had separated the list by property owners that were identified as individuals first, then there was a break in the list for corporations.

Three corporations, but the other two were well-known companies. One was owned by an insurance company, which he found odd. The second was owned by the Herbert Kohlmann Foundation, which he also found interesting.

But the third was Investments, Inc.

He reached for his newly charged-up disposable phone. "Gabe? It's Flynn. I need you to dig into Investments, Inc."

"I started looking into that one," Gabe admitted. "But so far I haven't found much. It was created three years ago, which is about when the house on Peabody Lake was purchased."

"And how long has Steve Miller been the CEO of Brookland Bank?" he asked.

"Three years, why?" Gabe asked. "Oh, you think they're related?"

Flynn had no idea what to think. "Maybe. The timing is suspicious enough."

"I'll see what I can come up with," Gabe promised.

"Thanks. Later, Gabe." He disconnected from the call, still thinking about the property on Peabody Lake and the three-year time frame of Steve Miller being the president of the bank.

Cassidy arrived twenty minutes later. "Hey, I heard about how you went swimming in Peabody Lake. Are you okay now?"

"Yeah, we're fine." He felt like an idiot for putting himself and Taylor in that position in the first place. "Thankfully, Rhy came through for us."

"He always does," Cassidy agreed with a smile. "Are you guys ready? We should hit the road."

Glancing at his watch, he realized they only had thirty minutes to get out to Ravenswood. Normally, it was only a twenty-minute ride, but he hated to keep Brady waiting.

"Okay, we're ready." Rhy had purchased two winter coats for them, which was nice. He found Taylor's and held it out for her. "Nice to have one that's dry, huh?"

"Yes, and I'm glad you have one too." She flipped her hair over her collar as Cassidy reached for the door handle. "Thanks for coming with us."

"Anytime." Cassidy opened the door, glanced outside, then gestured for them to follow. "Let's go."

Flynn knew it was likely overkill to have Cassidy along for the ride, but he would rather be safe than sorry. He had his gun tucked into his coat pocket, although he suspected he would not be allowed to bring the weapon inside the FBI offices. Normally, he would have wanted to take the time to clean and oil the weapon, but there hadn't been time.

At least Cass was armed too. He didn't argue when she slid in behind the wheel, quickly opening the back passenger door for Taylor.

They were on the road less than a minute later. He

couldn't seem to relax, turning to glance frequently through the rear window.

"I made sure I wasn't followed," Cass said, a slight edge to her tone. "I backtracked twice."

"Sorry." He tried to settle down. "I trust you. It's just been a little hairy over the past few hours."

"Rhy mentioned how you lost the boat." Cass glanced at him. "He had a budget meeting with the assistant chief this afternoon."

"I heard." He did his best to shrug off the guilt. Rhy hadn't blamed him for the incident, but that didn't mean his boss wouldn't take heat for the budget variance. Replacing a boat didn't cost any less than replacing a damaged car. The only good news was that the boat was small and used. Not a large speedboat like the one the gunman was using.

"Did you find anything interesting in the list of property owners?" Cass asked. "Gabe told me he sent it to you."

He filled her in on Investments, Inc. "The only reason it caught my attention was because of the Brookland Bank angle," he admitted. "It will be interesting to see if the feds can dig up anything more about the company."

"I'm sure they will." Cass waved a hand. "That's their job, right? I think Gabe has spoken to the Bureau tech guy, Ian, a time or two."

Two nerds bonding over data, Flynn thought with a smile. Cassidy talked about Gabe as if he was just one of the guys, unlike the way Gabe seemed to hang on to her every word.

Not my business, he reminded himself. He turned to glance at Taylor, then narrowed his gaze at Cassidy's knowing smile.

He caught the sign indicating they'd reached the city of

Ravenswood. "The FBI office building isn't far from Lake Michigan," he said for Taylor's benefit. "Must be nice."

"I don't get the impression they have much time to enjoy the view," Cass said. "That's the building up ahead."

"I see it." He leaned forward raking his gaze over the parking lot. There were a few cameras mounted on the structure if you knew where to look for them.

He used his new phone to call Brady. Rhy had been nice enough to program his brother's name and number into the device. "We're here," he said.

"I'll be out in a second."

Cassidy pulled into the closest parking space to the main entrance. He pushed out of his seat at the same time Cassidy did. Then he opened Taylor's door. "Stay close to me, okay?"

She nodded but didn't seem worried. He waited for Brady to come out of the building before escorting her around the front of the car.

A crack of gunfire had him throwing himself on top of Taylor.

His heart thundered in his chest as he waited for the next bullet to strike.

CHAPTER TEN

Taylor's hands and knees stung from hitting the asphalt parking lot. With Flynn's body draped over hers and Cassidy crouched beside her, she couldn't see a thing. But she had heard the gunfire.

"Get her inside! Hurry!"

She didn't recognize the male voice but wasn't surprised when Flynn answered. "No way. We're getting her out of here."

"The shooter is still out there," the male voice protested. She realized the voice belonged to Rhy's brother Brady. She'd remembered seeing the blond-haired guy coming out of the building. "I have agents scouring the parking lot, and I understand your concern about being found here, but for now, you need to bring Taylor inside."

"He's right, Flynn," Cassidy said. "We'd be sitting ducks in the SUV."

"Fine." Flynn sounded upset, but the pressure of his body over hers eased back. "But we'll cover her all the way."

"Of course," Cassidy murmured. Flynn rose as Brady joined them. Flynn and Brady towered over her, but

Cassidy wasn't as tall as she reached for her arm. "Can you stand?"

"Yes." She told herself this wasn't the time to fall apart. That she needed to keep it together long enough to reach the relative safety of the building.

Then the impact of Brady's comment sank in. How had they been found here? Federal agents had asked to interview her. The same agents, she assumed, who were working the double homicide as it relates to the banking industry.

A shiver rippled over her, one that had nothing to do with the crisp November air. She huddled close to Flynn and Cassidy as they moved together toward the building.

Less than two minutes later, she stood in a vestibule between two sets of doors. Brady pressed his ID against a badge reader, unlocking the second set of doors.

"I don't like this," Flynn said as they entered the building. They stopped in front of a desk manned by an agent. Three visitor badges were already on top of the desk waiting for them. Flynn grabbed one, then offered her and Cassidy the other two before turning back to Brady. "Where's your boss, the special agent in charge? I think he needs to know about the leak inside the agency."

"Presumed leak," Brady said, sounding a bit testy. "It could be that you were followed here."

"We weren't followed," Cassidy said. "I agree with Flynn on this one. The FBI asked for this interview, then someone takes a shot at Taylor. The connection is obvious."

Brady sighed heavily. "Okay, let's get you situated in a conference room. I'll update Donovan."

Taylor was ushered through another set of doors and into a hallway. Brady turned into the first door on the left, indicating the rest of them should follow. The room consisted of a long table, several chairs, a phone, and a computer with a large screen mounted on one end of the room. She dropped into the closest chair, rubbing her hands over her knees. Her new jeans hadn't been ripped, but there were likely bruises already forming beneath the fabric.

Better than being dead, she thought grimly.

"I need to know if your agents find anything related to the shooter," Flynn said.

He and Brady eyed each other for a long moment before Brady nodded. "I understand your need to stay informed. But this is technically a Bureau case now."

"Not until I'm convinced someone inside the Bureau isn't dirty," Flynn shot back. "I won't let anyone get to Taylor."

Brady sighed again, but surprisingly, he didn't argue. Taylor was relieved when Flynn took one seat beside her, while Cassidy sat on her other side, so that she was sandwiched between them.

After Brady left, Cassidy leaned forward to look at Flynn. "I'm certain I wasn't followed."

"I believe you," Flynn said. "I know Brady and Doug are good agents, but I'm not sure I trust whoever these guys are that want to interview Taylor."

She glanced between the two of them. "I'm no expert, but it doesn't seem logical that a dirty FBI agent would have the shooter show up here where it's more obvious that they might be implicated."

Flynn frowned, then nodded. "That's a good point. But how were we found here if there isn't an inside leak?"

She didn't have an answer for that.

Cassidy did, though. "It could be that the same man who hired the gunman to get rid of Steve and Robin Miller knew the feds would be involved. And that they'd want to talk to the only witness to the murders. So he sent the gunman here to wait for us to show."

Flynn grimaced, then nodded. "I can buy that theory. But I don't plan to trust the feds until we know for sure one way or the other."

Cassidy shrugged. "I understand your concern, but we need to consider the possibility that if the agents are clean, they have more resources to use when it comes to protecting Taylor. Specifically, a safe house."

"We're on the list for the MPD safe house," Flynn said. Again, she felt like a spectator at a tennis match, her gaze bouncing from Flynn to Cassidy, then back to Flynn.

"I know, Rhy mentioned that." Cassidy glanced over as the door to the conference room opened, revealing Brady and an older man with dark hair flecked with gray at the temples.

"Ms. Templeton? I'm Donovan, the special agent in charge. I understand you had an incident outside the building."

"MPD Officer Flynn Ryerson." Flynn rose to his feet. "I appreciate you coming to speak with us."

"I'm MPD Officer Cassidy Sommer," Cassidy added, also standing. "I can attest to the fact that we were not followed. The shooter was positioned north of the building. The weapon didn't sound like a rifle to me. I believe he was using a handgun."

"I have agents scouring the area," Donovan said. "I don't like knowing Ms. Templeton was targeted here. I want to assure you that my agents are clean. I don't have any reason to suspect any of them of being involved."

There was a long moment of silence as Flynn seemed to wrestle with a response. "I don't want to believe anyone here is involved, but we haven't spoken to anyone but Rhy and Brady. Your agents asked for this interview."

"I agree that it looks suspicious," Donovan said, looking surprisingly weary. "I find it hard to believe a dirty agent would be so bold, or stupid, to attempt to shoot a witness in front of the office building."

Taylor had risen to her feet, too, but glanced around warily at Flynn, Cassidy, Brady, and the special agent in charge.

It seemed as if they might be at a stalemate.

"I'm happy to do the interview," she finally said. "But I would like to know how we'll get out of here when that's finished. I want to stay with Flynn and Cassidy, and we need some assurances that we'll be able to leave safely."

Flynn didn't look totally happy with her comment, but he didn't argue. After a long moment, Donovan gave a curt nod. "I will provide an armed escort when it's time for you to leave."

Flynn scowled. "That only works if the vehicles are driven by you, Brady, and/or Doug. No one else."

"That will be arranged," Donovan said. Taylor was impressed he was being so cooperative. "Now I would like to allow Bureau agents Sally Fisk and Travis Goldberg to come in and speak with you."

"I'm ready." Taylor was anxious to get this part over with.

Brady hung back after Donovan left. "I'll call Rhy," he said in a low tone. "We'll arrange for a rendezvous location to swap vehicles once we leave here."

"Thanks, Brady," Flynn said. "I hate to be a jerk, but Taylor has been under attack since the Millers were murdered."

"I understand." Brady stepped back as the two agents

entered the conference room. Then after giving her a quick nod, he stepped out, leaving the five of them alone.

"Ms. Templeton? I'm Travis, and this is my partner, Sally." Agent Travis Goldberg stepped forward to shake her hand. Agent Sally Fisk did the same. Flynn and Cassidy introduced themselves, too, making it clear they were staying for the duration of the interview.

When the introductions were complete, Sally and Travis took seats on the opposite side of the table. From there, the interview went exactly as she'd expected.

Did she know anything about Steve Miller's bank? No. Did she know the shooter? No. Had she ever seen Nickoli Yurgis before the night of the shooting? No. Did she have any idea why the Millers had been targeted? No.

On and on and on.

It was only after she'd finished recounting the night of the murders that the two agents turned their attention to Flynn and Cassidy.

Mostly Flynn.

During the interview, Flynn's icy attitude had thawed toward the agents. Maybe in part because they were clearly interested in his opinion regarding the various attempts against her.

"The way the gunman—who we believe is Nickoli Yurgis—found us on Peabody Lake, then again here at the FBI building has me wondering who has hired him," Flynn said. "It feels like the mastermind behind this has deep pockets. Not just financial resources, but a way to connect with professional hit men too."

"Tell us again about the property you found on Peabody Lake?" Sally Fisk asked. "What was the company called?"

"Investments, Inc." Flynn gestured to the computer screen on the wall. "You might want to bring up a map of the lake, see if we can pinpoint the location of the property owned by the corporation. I might be able to tell you if it's the same one where the photograph of Lyle and Jake Paulson was taken."

Travis pulled out his phone. "Ian? We need your expertise in the conference room. Thanks."

Taylor remembered something about a tech guy named Ian who had a similar role as Gabe Melrose. Ian arrived with a laptop, booted it up, and then somehow projected the laptop screen onto the bigger one.

"Peabody Lake, property owned by Investments, Inc." Ian spoke to himself as he worked the computer. Taylor had to give him credit, he was able to bring up the address onto the screen, then used a map application to zoom in on the home.

She gasped at the image on the screen. Glancing at Flynn, she saw he was staring in shock too.

There was no doubt that the house on the screen was the same one where her cousins had been photographed.

And likely the one belonging to the individual who had orchestrated the murders.

FLYNN DIDN'T FEEL the sense of satisfaction he thought he would at being proven right. Maybe in part because he was still a bit shaken over the gunfire attempt outside the Bureau. He forced himself to concentrate on the case.

"That's the house." He nodded at the screen. "Taylor and I were on the boat and recognized that deck as being where the picture of Lyle and Jake Paulson was taken. We were heading back to our rental property when we saw the speedboat racing toward us. Unfortunately, I cannot say with certainty that the boat came from that property." He gestured to the screen. "But he was clearly determined to eliminate us. He opened fire, sinking our boat and sending us swimming toward shore."

"Surprised you didn't succumb to hypothermia," Sally said with a frown.

"We almost did." Flynn knew that God had spared their lives. That was the only explanation as to how they'd gotten out of the lake in time. "Can you get a search warrant for the property? Dig deeper into who really owns it?"

The two feds glanced at each other. "Not sure about a search warrant," Travis said. "We don't have probable cause, especially since you can't identify the shooter as coming from that location. But digging into the ownership is absolutely something Ian can do."

"I'll work on that," Ian agreed. "But at first glance, it's not going to be easy. Looks like this company is owned by another company."

Sally drummed her fingers on the table. "I thought we had new rules that went into effect this year to prevent hiding the true owners of corporations?"

"We do," Ian said. "But that doesn't mean everyone has complied. And depending on how far behind the bureaucrats are, they may not have gotten around to following up with those who didn't cooperate."

Flynn bit back a sarcastic response. There was no reason to point out that it wasn't the least bit surprising that government rules were rarely followed by criminals.

He stared at the house on the screen. Maybe they didn't have probable cause for a search warrant, but they could still walk up to the door and knock.

"We'll head over there," Travis said as if reading his

mind. "Maybe someone will answer the door. And we can talk to the neighbors, too, see if we learn anything that way."

He nodded. "I like that idea. Maybe the neighbors don't appreciate having a house owned by a corporation. Could be that different people are staying there throughout the year."

"Exactly," Travis agreed. "Anything else you think might help?"

He considered that for a moment. "I returned fire on the speedboat, and I know I hit the vessel. I'm not sure how badly it was damaged, though. If you do get someone to answer the door, you might want to ask to see the boat on the property. Finding a bullet hole in the vessel would give you the probable cause you need to search the house."

"Can't hurt to try," Sally said, making a note. "I doubt we'll get that much cooperation, but again, the neighbors might have seen something suspicious."

A tiny flame of hope flickered in his heart. Maybe the investigation would get some traction with the feds working the case. He thought again about the banking aspect. "Have you uncovered unusual activity within Brookland Bank?"

"Not yet, but we're working on that," Travis said. "We have to go through some red tape to get the access we need."

Of course, they did, he thought with a sigh. Nothing was ever easy. "Will you let us know if you find something?" Sensing a lack of enthusiasm to share information from the pair of agents, he added, "Maybe Taylor will remember some snippet of conversation if you find something specific."

Travis Goldberg scratched his chin. "Okay, sure. We'll keep you in the loop."

"We'll need your contact information," Sally said.

"No, you can reach us through Brady Finnegan,"

Cassidy said, joining the conversation for the first time. "I'm sure you can understand the need to keep Ms. Templeton off-grid."

Travis's face flushed. "Despite what happened outside, we are not the bad guys here. We did not leak any information about this interview. We didn't even know anything about this case until a few hours ago."

Flynn held the agent's gaze. "I understand your perspective, but what would you think in our shoes?" He leaned forward. "There have been multiple attacks against Ms. Templeton in the past few hours. We just met you. You can't expect instant trust."

Sally grimaced and nodded. "Okay, okay. Let's call a truce. As Travis said, we're not the bad guys. But you have a right to be wary. If we need to speak with Ms. Templeton again, or if we uncover additional information, we will go through Finnegan to reach you."

"Thanks," Cassidy said.

"Yes, thanks." Flynn decided it would be best to smooth things over. "We appreciate everything you're doing on this."

Mollified, Travis rose and offered his hand. Flynn accepted the handshake peace offering, as did Taylor and Cassidy. After they all bid their goodbyes, the two agents and Ian the tech expert all left the room.

Brady appeared a moment later. "How did it go?"

"Surprisingly well," Flynn had to admit. He was finding it difficult to imagine Travis and Sally as dirty cops. Maybe he was being naïve, but they came across as earnest and anxious to get to the bottom of this nightmare. "They're heading out to Peabody Lake to see if anyone is at the residence."

"And to talk to the neighbors," Cassidy said. "I have a

feeling that will be their best way to get information." She grinned. "You know how nosy some neighbors are."

Brady laughed. "True." Then his expression turned somber. "Rhy, Doug, and I have a plan to get you out of here."

"Glad to hear it." Flynn was relieved to have support from the Finnegan family. Doug Bridges was also a great guy to have on their side. Bridges had been instrumental in helping Roscoe protect Libby a few months ago.

He trusted these men and women with his life and, more importantly, with Taylor's too.

"We'll take my car out of here," Brady said, leading them through the building. Flynn noticed they were not heading out the main doors where they'd come in. "We'll leave the vehicle you arrived in out front. Doug has his vehicle, too, and he'll leave ahead of us." He frowned, then added, "I thought for now we'd rendezvous with Rhy at the City Central Hotel. I've asked Bax Scala to reserve the suite through the DA's office."

Flynn glanced at Taylor who eyed him curiously. "Is that the same City Central Hotel we stayed in with Sienna, Bailey, and Zeke?"

"Yeah, it is." Flynn had been grazed by a bullet there too. "I know the plan was to avoid going back there, and they wouldn't likely want us back either, but with the room being registered by the DA's office, we should have the anonymity we need."

"Bax is our brother-in-law," Brady explained. "He's also the assistant district attorney. They use the City Central for witnesses all the time."

"From there, we'll find somewhere else to go," Flynn added, when Taylor still looked concerned. "We just need a temporary meeting place."

Brady hesitated outside a door that appeared to have an alarm built in. "Ready?" He used his ID badge to disarm the security system. "Doug is outside waiting for us."

Flynn nodded, his gut tightening as Brady pushed through the door. Cassidy went next. He nudged Taylor to follow Cass, sticking close behind her.

Doug was indeed standing outside in the cold. He gestured to the two vehicles parked within a short distance of the door. "Let's go."

A few minutes later, they were out on the street, leaving the Bureau via the back exit. Flynn and Taylor were in the back seat, and he scanned the area as Brady drove.

There was nothing to see. No surprise the shooter had vanished as quickly as he'd popped up.

"Do you really think agents Travis and Sally will let us know what they find out?" Taylor asked. "I always heard the feds weren't good about cooperating with local cops."

"Hey, I always cooperate with the locals," Brady said defensively. "We get a bad rap because of a few TV shows."

Taylor flushed. "Yeah, sorry. I have to admit that until today I've never met a federal agent in person."

"It's fine." Brady waved a hand. "I'm sure there were jerk agents at some point to start the rumor."

"I would like to think they'll keep us in the loop," Flynn said, getting the conversation back on track. "That's why I added the part about the possibility of you remembering something important if prodded by additional information."

"Yeah, well, don't hold your breath on that," she muttered. "I was the nanny; my job was to take care of the baby." Her brow furrowed. "I really hope Max is okay."

Flynn reached out to take her hand. "He'll be fine."

She shook her head. "You don't know that."

That was true, he didn't know where Max was or what

sort of foster family he had been placed with. "We'll pray for him, okay?"

Her fingers tightened around his. "I'd like that."

"Dear Lord Jesus, keep baby Max safe in Your care. Amen," Flynn said.

"Amen," Cassidy, Brady, and Taylor echoed in unison.

Taylor clung to his hand during the rest of the trip to the City Central Hotel, and he was in no hurry to let her go. Flynn noticed Brady's knowing smile when their gazes met in the rearview mirror.

So much for his attempt to keep Taylor at a distance. If anything, the recent shooting attempt had drawn them closer together.

He was fighting a losing battle. Despite the mistakes he'd made along the way, of which there were many, he couldn't step aside to let someone else take over the task of protecting her.

Not even those men he deeply admired, like Rhy, Brady, and Doug Bridges.

Up ahead he could see Doug driving slowly enough that they could stick close. Daytime traffic wasn't too bad, and their rush hour was nothing compared to other big cities.

But he was relieved when they finally reached the City Central Hotel. Doug parked his SUV in the front lot, but Brady went around back. When he caught Flynn's curious glance, he said, "Doug is going to get the room keys. Then he'll open the back door for us. He'll eventually park in the back too. Rhy will join us after his meeting with Michaels."

"Sounds good." The feds had implemented the plan to get them away from Ravenswood very well. When Bridges appeared in the doorway, they quickly worked together to escort Taylor inside.

"I see they made repairs to the drywall since we were here last," Taylor said as she flopped onto the sofa.

Brady arched a brow, but Flynn ignored the unspoken question. "Are you hungry? Thirsty? We can order something from room service."

"No thanks. We can grab dinner later." She yawned, then said, "Maybe coffee. I don't normally drink this much coffee, but I am surprisingly exhausted.

"That's adrenaline for you," Cassidy said. "I'll make coffee."

"I feel like having everyone hovering here is overkill." Taylor frowned at Doug and Brady standing on either side of the door like sentinels guarding a post. "Don't you guys have criminals to catch?"

"I have a feeling that finding Nickoli Yurgis will be a huge step forward in uncovering other criminals," Flynn said. "And I promised we'd keep you safe."

"I know." She abruptly jumped off the sofa and headed to the closest bedroom. "Excuse me."

He took a step after her, then stopped. Each room had an attached bathroom. She was obviously looking for some privacy.

But after one minute passed, then five, then ten, he grew concerned. He shot Cassidy a panicked look.

"I'll check on her," Cass offered.

"No, let me." He couldn't explain why he brushed past Cass to knock on the bedroom door, then he cracked it open. "Taylor? Are you okay?"

No answer. He opened the door farther. Seeing her curled in a ball on the bed sobbing was like a knife to the chest.

CHAPTER ELEVEN

Everything caught up with her in one fell swoop. Taylor was exhausted, emotionally and physically. It was all too much. The attacks against her flashed in her mind, one after the other like snippets from a movie reel. Hearing the *pop, pop, pop, pop*. The gunman walking past the bedroom door, then playing his flashlight across the room. The gunman taking shots at their SUV after leaving the Brookland Police Department, then finding them at the rental property and forcing them to drive through the garage door to escape. The boat incident on Peabody Lake, suffering hypothermia and nearly drowning.

And lastly the shooting outside the FBI building.

Worst of all, the knowledge that this all started with the brutal murders of her second cousins, Steve and Robin Miller, along with her cousin Roman Paulson. The DNA link was disturbing in more ways than one.

It all came back to her family being involved. Distant family, maybe, but still family. *Why, Lord, why?*

There was no answer from above.

"Taylor, please don't cry." A warm hand rested on her

shoulder. She belatedly realized Flynn had come into the room to find her.

She struggled to pull herself together. It wasn't easy. The dam holding back her tears had opened, and she couldn't figure out how to slam it shut.

"I'm here. You're safe. I promise I'll do everything possible to keep you safe." His voice sounded tortured, as if he was just as upset.

Somehow, she managed to stop crying. She took one breath, then another, slowing her breathing to the point where she could speak. "I know that." Her voice was muffled against the pillow, so she said it again, louder this time. "I know that." She wiped her face with the pillowcase, then lifted her head. "It's been a long day."

"Too long," he agreed, smoothing his hand down her back in a sweet gesture. "But please don't give up hope."

A Bible verse from the book of Psalms flashed in her mind from her last church service. Something about hope. What was it? *For in thee, O Lord, do I hope: thou wilt hear, O Lord my God (Psalms 38:15).*

Amazingly, a sense of peace washed over her. She and Flynn were not alone in this nightmare. Here on earth they had support from the Finnegans, Doug Bridges, Cassidy, and other members of the tactical team who were determined to protect them.

But over and above that, they had God with them. She felt the Lord's presence now more than ever before.

She swallowed hard and nodded. Then she sat all the way up, moving over to give Flynn room to sit on the edge of the bed beside her. "I haven't given up hope. I just—lost it for a minute. Everything that has taken place of the last few hours weighed down on me to the point I suddenly felt overwhelmed."

"That's understandable." A frown furrowed his brow. "I hate knowing how badly I'm failing you."

"You're not." She drummed up a weak smile. "You've been great. Truly."

"Says the woman who was sobbing her heart out a minute ago," he said with a wry grimace.

She reached over to take his hand. "I'm fine. Thanks to you, Flynn. The way you threw yourself over me when the gunfire rang out? That was true courage."

He tucked a strand of her blond hair behind her ear. "It was instinct, not courage. I'm trained to put myself in harm's way. Any of my teammates would have done the same thing."

She knew it was more than skill and training. Maybe all cops reacted like that instinctively. Yet, she knew Flynn would protect her with his life. No matter what. She managed a smile. "Maybe I lost focus for a minute, as the situation outside the FBI building hit hard, but I know God is watching over us. With the Lord's help, we'll get through this."

He nodded slowly, his green eyes intent as their gazes caught and held. In a nanosecond, the atmosphere in the room changed. A keen awareness abruptly sizzled in the air between them. She found herself leaning closer, even as he did the same, dropping his head so that their mouths met halfway.

His kiss was tentative at first, but then deepened as he drew her close. The synapses in her brain went haywire, and everything faded except for Flynn.

His strength. His warmth. His woodsy scent. And the way he kissed her as if he'd never get enough.

A feeling she shared wholeheartedly.

She slipped her arms around his waist, turning into his

embrace. Being with Flynn like this was amazing, and she wanted nothing more than to sit there kissing him forever.

But, of course, that was impossible. It seemed like mere seconds had passed when there was a sharp knock on the door. She wanted to pretend she didn't hear it, but then the knock came again.

"Flynn? Taylor? Everything all right?" Cassidy asked.

Flynn abruptly ended their kiss at the sound of Cassidy's voice. The way his breath came unevenly made her feel good to know she wasn't the only one impacted from their embrace.

She wanted to pull him in for another kiss, but he glanced toward the door.

"Fine," Flynn said gruffly. He cleared his throat, then added, "Everything is fine. Be out in a sec."

She ducked her head, hiding a smile. He continued holding her for a long moment, then reluctantly released her. "I need to get back out there to discuss our next steps."

"I understand." The reality of the situation was sobering. This wasn't the time to be kissing Flynn. Not when there was a professional hit man with ties to the Russian Mafia set on killing her. Running her fingers through her hair, she rose to her feet. "I'll join you in a few minutes."

Flynn's smile was sweet. "Take your time."

She ducked into the bathroom, nearly groaning out loud when she saw how awful she looked. No pretty crying for her, the way actresses in movies looked so beautiful when they were emotionally distraught. Her nose was red, her eyes puffy and swollen. Her hair was a tangled mess and damp from her tears.

Why on earth had Flynn kissed her?

Or had she kissed him?

She felt certain she wasn't alone in feeling the attraction

between them, but Flynn had been quick to pull away. As if he did not want Cassidy to know how close they'd gotten.

Whatever. It didn't matter. Shaking her head at her foolishness, she splashed cold water on her face. Then she took a moment to press a washcloth soaked in cold water against her eyes. After blowing her nose and drying her face, she looked in the mirror, relieved she looked better. Not great, but not as bad as before.

Note to self, she thought with a sigh, *no more crying*.

The truth was she didn't normally lose control like that. Obviously, what she'd been through over the past— what, fourteen hours?—were far from normal circum- stances. Most nannies took care of kids without catching a glimpse of a professional hit man leaving the scene of a double homicide while protecting the children under their care.

She still felt sick remembering how close she and Max had come to being killed that night. If she hadn't texted Flynn when she had, if he hadn't called 911 on her behalf and broken speed records to get there . . .

Best not to think about it. She was alive and so was Max. She wanted to see the baby for herself once this was over to make sure he was okay.

But that would only happen once the danger was over.

As she emerged from the bedroom, Flynn, Cassidy, Doug, and Brady all glanced at her. She did her best to smile as she crossed over to sit on the sofa between Flynn and Cassidy. "Okay, what's the plan?"

There was a brief moment of silence before Brady took the lead. He and Doug were sitting at the small kitchen table, facing them. Brady gave her a slight nod as he spoke. "Rhy is on his way, so we're waiting to take action until he gets here to see what he thinks. We've gone through the shooting incident again, but I need to ask you if there's anything you can tell us about that?"

"Me?" She echoed in surprise. She glanced at Flynn, then shook her head. "I'm sorry but no. I heard the gunfire, then Flynn was pushing me to the ground, covering me." She thought back for a moment. "I didn't see anything suspicious before that."

Brady nodded as if he'd expected that answer. "I had to ask, just in case you noticed something small that we didn't. None of us caught a glimpse of the shooter either. Although I'm certain it's the same one you have already identified, Nickoli Yurgis." He shrugged. "At this point, we've decided against using one of the FBI safe houses, so it looks like we're stuck with either motels or rental properties."

She nodded, knowing Flynn was likely the one who'd nixed the idea of using an FBI safe house. The agents who'd interviewed her had been respectful and came across as good cops intent on finding the shooter.

But she also understood that Flynn was unwilling to trust anyone outside of the Finnegan and tactical team family. Doug Bridges being the sole exception.

"Nothing yet on the company that owns the house on Peabody Lake?" she asked. Her gaze darted from Brady to Doug Bridges. Both men wore somber expressions as if they were feeling the magnitude of the shooting outside the FBI building too. "Your tech guy was going to work on that, right?"

"Yes, Ian is digging into the ownership of the corporation," Doug said with a nod. "I know he'll be in touch the minute he finds anything."

"I also left Gabe a message," Flynn added. "He's working on identifying those involved in forming the company too."

"They're both talented guys," Brady said. "I'm sure they'll find something useful."

Should, could, hopefully . . . she tried not to feel depressed about the lack of progress on the case. Everyone was working hard. It wasn't that they weren't trying.

Yet deep down, she felt sick. If the FBI and the local police couldn't find the shooter, who could?

FLYNN AVOIDED Cass's knowing gaze. He didn't like to think the fact that he'd been kissing Taylor was written all over his face, but the way she'd eyed him suspiciously convinced him it must be obvious.

If someone cared to look.

Thankfully, the guys were more concerned with the case and the task of protecting Taylor. She didn't look very happy to hear they didn't have much of anything to go on. And he couldn't blame her.

He'd hoped they'd have identified a solid plan by now. Part of that was waiting for Rhy to get there.

"I think we should stay away from motels that have been associated with the tactical team or the feds," Brady said. He waved a hand at the room. "That means moving out of here sooner than later."

"And go where?" Flynn demanded. "We tried a rental house secured under Gabe's name, but that didn't work. If we can't use federal resources or local cop resources, how are we going to arrange for a place to stay?"

"I don't know," Brady admitted. "I'm trying to think of someone we know well enough that would pay for a place under their name but who also wouldn't be obviously connected to us."

"My younger half sister can do it," Doug said. "She lives out of state in Jackson, Wyoming, and her last name is Sanders. Emily Sanders."

"Really?" Flynn stared at Bridges. "You don't mind asking her for a favor?"

Doug shrugged. "Of course not. She won't mind and knows I'll pay her back once this is over."

"We'll pay you back," Flynn swiftly added. "Don't worry about that. This isn't your fight, it's ours. And thank you, I really appreciate the offer."

Brady's phone rang. He glanced at the screen. "This is Rhy." He stood and moved to a quiet corner of the room. "Hey, bro. How did it go?"

Flynn thought about Doug Bridges's half sister arranging a rental house for them. Unless Rhy could get them into the MPD safe house, that was their best option. He glanced at Taylor who looked encouraged by the plan too.

Although keeping Taylor safe was only half the battle. They really needed something more than just the gunman to connect the three murders of Steve and Robin Miller and Roman Paulson.

The house on Peabody Lake was key. If they could figure out who owned it, then they'd be one step closer to unraveling the case.

Or so he hoped. As much as he hated to admit it, police work was rarely that easy.

"Okay, Rhy is parking in the back of the hotel," Brady announced. "I'll go let him in."

They sat in silence for a few minutes until Rhy and Brady returned. Rhy looked on edge, and Flynn had a bad feeling his meeting with Michaels didn't go as well as Rhy had hoped.

"Everything okay?" Flynn asked.

Rhy grimaced. "Yeah, nothing new." He waved a hand as if the meeting with the upper brass was nothing to be concerned about. "I'll survive."

"We're here for you," Flynn said. "I know you stick your neck out for us on a regular basis. Whatever you need, we'll do our part."

Rhy managed a smile as he dropped into the chair Brady had vacated. "I know, thanks. Okay, on to bigger issues. How on earth did our gunman, Yurgis, find you outside the FBI building?"

"There are only two viable scenarios," Flynn said. "Either someone within the FBI is a part of this mess and on the payroll or the gunman assumed the feds would want to talk to Taylor, so he camped out there and waited for us."

Rhy scowled. "I don't know if this guy is smart enough to stake the place out."

"We spoke to SAC Donovan; he doesn't think any of the agents are involved," Brady said. "But you know how that goes. He'll need some sort of evidence indicating that before he'll take that possibility seriously."

"Even though he already knows what happened back when Roscoe and Libby were hiding from the cartel?" Flynn asked. "That someone high up in the DEA was involved?"

Brady frowned. "You're thinking Donovan is the mole?"

"I didn't say that," Flynn protested. "But after what went down back in July, your boss should be more open to the possibility of someone operating against us from the inside."

There was a moment of silence as everyone considered that. Then Doug spoke up. "If you want me to call my sister to make the arrangements for another rental property, I need to do that soon. She's a nurse and sometimes works night shift. If she's sleeping, she won't answer the phone, but she'll return my call when she wakes up."

"Your sister?" Rhy looked surprised. "All this time we've been working together, and I never knew you had family in the area."

"She lives in Jackson, Wyoming," Doug said. "Her last name is different from mine, which should give us the anonymity we need." He held up his phone. "I'll make some calls if you're on board with that plan."

Rhy nodded. "Unfortunately, the MPD safe house is still in use. And after hearing about the shooting at the FBI office, I'm loathe to use anything with MPD or FBI connections. A rental property secured under your sister's name sounds like a good option."

"Great. I'll see what I can do." Doug moved away to make the calls. Thankfully, it didn't take too long. "Thanks, Em. If you can find a house in the Brookland or Greenland area, that would be great. Talk to you soon." He turned back to face them. "Emily is searching for viable options."

"Why did you tell her to focus on Brookland and Greenland?" Cassidy asked.

Doug shrugged. "I keep going back to how the president and CEO of the Brookland Bank was shot and killed. He must be the key to all of this."

A strange thought occurred to Flynn. "Even if Taylor hadn't been at the house as a witness to the murders, a bank president shot in his bed at night is sure to garner attention. Specifically from the feds if they think there's international money fraud involved." He glanced from Taylor to Cassidy, back to Rhy and Brady. "I don't understand why the killer didn't at least try to make their deaths look like an accident."

"That's a good question. Maybe Steve Miller was set up

to take the fall," Rhy said thoughtfully. "Plus, accidents have a way of backfiring. Either someone sees something they shouldn't or the accident doesn't kill the target outright as planned."

"But that line of thinking does lead us back to someone within the FBI being involved," Cassidy said. "The goal may have been for the guy on the inside to make sure the investigation doesn't get solved."

Brady leaned against the counter, pursing his lips. "I hate thinking someone I work with is involved in this. I've been there for years and can't imagine anyone stooping so low. As long as we are considering all options, though, I feel the need to point out that if my boss, Donovan, is the bad guy, he might know about Doug's sister."

"Maybe not," Flynn said. "I had considered that possibility too. Doug works for the DEA, right? That's a different division of the federal government."

"True, but they're all housed in our building," Brady said. "And Donovan has access to our personal records."

That gave him pause. He glanced at Doug, who shrugged. "Up to you. Although I don't know of anyone else who can do the rental for us."

Flynn didn't know of anyone else they could use either. He'd thought briefly about asking Sienna's new manager to assist, but the incident last month when Zeke was shot and injured was all over the news, so he decided against that. Who else? His family lived up in Green Bay, but he didn't want to put them in danger either.

"I don't have any reason not to trust my boss," Brady said, breaking the long silence. "Back when my son was kidnapped, he was supportive of me and the other agents working the case. He's never so much as taken a paper clip from the Bureau and always comes across as dedicated to upholding the law." Brady spread his hands wide. "I wouldn't even be going down this path except for the way you mentioned the situation with Roscoe. We'd be foolish not to admit that anything is possible."

Flynn glanced at Taylor who had been quietly listening. "This impacts you the most, what would you like to do?"

She glanced around the room for a moment. Then sighed. "I don't know what we should do. It would be nice to stay here, but if that's not an option, then I think we should go along with heading to a rental property financed by Doug's sister, Emily." She hesitated, then added, "Honestly, if that doesn't work, then I'm not sure what will."

That gave them all pause. Because she was right. They really didn't know who exactly they were dealing with. Other than a professional hit man with ties to the Russian Mafia.

Was this related to political corruption? Money laundering? Or something else completely?

There was no way to narrow things down so they could focus the investigation on a specific issue. Not without knowing who owned the house on Peabody Lake.

And what if any connection did that person have with Taylor's cousins? Were they just friends? Colleagues?

Business partners?

No, the latter was too obvious. One guy killing off his business partners leaving him with all the assets would place him at the top of the suspect list. There had to be something else at play here.

What he wasn't sure.

Lack of sleep and nonstop thoughts of the case were making his head hurt. He was about to ask how soon they could get out of there when Bridges's phone rang.

"Hey, Em," Doug said, after lifting his phone to his ear. "Did you find something for me?"

The room fell silent as Doug listened and jotted notes.

"Great, thanks. We'll head there in an hour." Doug slipped the phone into his pocket. "Emily found a house in Greenland, directly across the street from the park. We can check in after four p.m."

"Good. I like the location near the park," Flynn said.

"Once we get you and Taylor situated in the rental property, I think Brady and I should drive past the Millers' home," Rhy said. "I can't lie, it bothers me that the murders happened so close to the homestead."

"You're not the target," Brady said. "But I get that Brookland doesn't see that level of criminal activity."

A hint of movement passed by the window to Flynn's right. For some reason, he jumped off the sofa and crossed the room, his weapon in his hand before he realized he'd drawn it.

"What's wrong?" Rhy quickly joined him, also holding his weapon. "Is someone out there?"

Flynn stood to the side and lifted the edge of the curtain to see better. This side of the suite overlooked the parking lot. He told himself he was overreacting, and when he peered out, he didn't see anyone.

Because he was hiding? There weren't that many places out there to avoid being seen, except for the smattering of cars in the lot.

"I think we should get Taylor out of here," he said. "Maybe it's nothing, but I don't want to take any more chances."

"We can't check into the rental yet," Doug said. "But I'm fine with getting out of here. We can take the scenic route out to Greenland."

"Stay with me, Taylor," Cassidy said, drawing Taylor off the sofa. Taylor glanced at him with fear in her eyes. "We'll cover you on the way outside."

"I'll go first," Doug said. "Brady, you bring Taylor, Flynn, and Cassidy. Rhy, you cover us from behind. All good?"

"Yep. Let's blow this pop stand," Brady said.

Doug opened the door, looked up and down the hall, then stepped out of the room. Brady went next. Flynn followed, indicating Taylor should stay behind him. Cassidy hovered behind her, leaving Rhy to cover their backs.

In single file, they made their way to the rear exit. Doug indicated they should stay back as he pushed open the door.

The sound of gunfire sent Doug and the rest of them down to the ground.

The movement passing their suite window hadn't been his imagination after all.

CHAPTER TWELVE

For the second time in less than three hours, Taylor dropped to the ground at the sound of gunfire. There were three pops, sounding much like the night of the original murders. From what she could tell, the gunfire came from outside the hotel.

How had the gunman known they were leaving? Or had he simply been sitting out there waiting for them to show?

Despite the danger, an odd sense of calmness washed over her. Maybe she was getting used to the sound of gunfire and being targeted by this guy because she wasn't worried.

Flynn and the others would get her out of there.

"Anyone hit?" Rhy asked. "Doug? Are you okay?"

"I'm good. But we need to move. I think the shooter is in the parking structure across the street. Flynn, get Taylor back in the room," Doug said in a terse tone. "Cassidy and Rhy, you go with them. Brady, come with me. We need to find this guy once and for all."

"I'll help you and Brady," Rhy said. "Flynn and Cassidy are more than capable of watching over Taylor."

She wanted to protest that none of them should leave the shelter of the building, but she wasn't the one in charge. She took a moment to thank God for His protection in watching over them as Flynn rose to a crouch and turned to look at her.

"You heard him. Let's go." Flynn's green eyes were sharp with anger.

After pushing herself up onto her hands and knees, she rose. Flynn and Cassidy shielded her exactly the way they had outside the FBI building. Sandwiched between them, they made their way back to the suite.

Flynn had a key card and used it to open the door. He brought his weapon up in a two-handed grip, the key card back in his pocket as he scanned the room. Then he glanced at Cassidy. "We need to sweep the place in case this was nothing more than a diversion."

"Agree." Cassidy gently nudged her across the threshold behind Flynn.

Once inside the room, Flynn gestured to the kitchenette. "Stay there, Taylor. This won't take long."

She nodded without saying anything. Some of her earlier calmness faded as she watched Cassidy and Flynn split up to search the two bedrooms.

It bothered her to watch Flynn face danger. She didn't like that for Cassidy either, but her gaze clung to Flynn as he flattened himself against the wall, peeked around the corner to scan the interior, then stepped inside the bedroom.

The room where they'd kissed less than an hour ago.

A wave of despair hit hard. What if Doug, Brady, and Rhy didn't find Nickoli Yurgis in the parking structure across the street?

If the gunman escaped, she felt certain he'd track her

down and fire at her again. Over and over until she was dead.

"Clear," Cassidy called.

"Clear," Flynn echoed.

Moments later, the two tactical team members returned to the main suite. Flynn walked to the window, peering outside.

"Have a seat on the sofa." Cassidy drew her over to it. "Better for you to sit here while keeping your head down."

She slouched in the corner of the sofa. "I don't hear anymore gunfire."

"I think our perp took off," Flynn said with disgust. "I'm not sure why he fired three shots in rapid succession like that. Anyone with half a brain would know that we wouldn't allow you to leave the building first."

"I was wondering about that too," Cassidy said with a frown. "I hate to give this guy too much credit, but it seems as if the shooter wanted to draw out Doug and Brady, while making sure the rest of us stayed put. Especially if he was firing from a position in the structure across the street."

"Tell me about it." Flynn's expression was grim. "The shadow passing by the window didn't have time to get all the way out to the parking structure across the street. So either I saw a local hotel patron or there's more going on. I plan to stay here, covering the window."

"Then I'll keep an eye on the main door," Cassidy said.

"Close the two bedroom doors first," Flynn said. "We need to be ready for anything. Especially another ambush. I wish we could lock the bedroom doors from this side, but I checked, and there's no way to do that."

Taylor shivered. Was this an attempt to divide and conquer? She'd assumed Nickoli Yurgis was acting on his own, but what if he had help? Not just from someone inside the FBI but also from another gunman?

Whoever had hired Nickoli could have easily dipped his hand into the pool of hired killers to find another. Especially if he or she had money to burn.

Why was it that bad guys who were rich always wanted to be richer? She truly didn't understand the mentality that a comfortable lifestyle wasn't enough.

A heavy silence hung between the three occupants of the room. She could tell that Cassidy and Flynn were listening and watching intently for someone to appear. Cassidy had her eye pressed against the peephole looking out into the hallway, while Flynn continually searched the area outside the window.

Taylor felt useless. Other than being curled in the corner of the sofa with her head down, she wasn't doing anything to help the situation.

She was only the cause of the situation.

The minutes passed with painful slowness. She imagined the three men outside, searching every nook and cranny for the gunman. When Flynn's phone rang, she startled badly, her heart nearly beating out of her chest. She glanced over to where Flynn was bringing the phone to his ear while still watching out the window. "Hey, Rhy. Did you find him?"

When Flynn's mouth flattened into a thin line, she knew the response wasn't reassuring.

"Okay, I guess it's good to know where he was and that he left a shell casing behind this time. That's progress and gives us something to work from. Hopefully, the crime scene techs can find more evidence." Flynn finally turned from the window to look over at her. "Yeah, I agree with the plan of getting Taylor out of here ASAP."

Cassidy turned from her position at the door. "The hallway is clear, and I hear sirens. That's our cue to hit the road."

Flynn nodded, still listening to Rhy. "Understood. We'll meet you out back."

Out back? The same place they'd been standing when the gunfire had erupted? Taylor swallowed hard, determined not to second guess the decision. These guys were the experts in this sort of thing.

She didn't know much of anything. Which was why it was so frustrating to be in this position. She was a nanny. Had a teaching degree. Enjoyed caring for kids.

Not hiding from danger.

"Yeah, I see you." Flynn had turned to look out the window again. "And we hear the sound of sirens as well. Best to get out of Dodge before we're stuck answering questions. Which vehicle was damaged?"

Taylor saw Cassidy wince at that. Remembering the conversation about budget issues for Rhy and the team, she understood the concern.

If she had money, she'd gladly pitch in. But she was still paying off her student loans.

"Yep. We're on our way." Flynn pocketed his phone, then crossed to the sofa. "We're taking Brady's car. Doug's SUV is damaged."

"Interesting that the fed's car was targeted," Cassidy said, peering through the peephole again before stepping back to open the door. "Almost as if the gunman knew which SUV to hit."

"It's hard to say for sure, there are three vehicles back there," Flynn said with a shrug. "Brady's SUV was first in line, then Doug's, and then Rhy's." He joined Cassidy at the door. "I'll take the lead. You cover Taylor from behind again, okay?"

"Yes," Cassidy agreed, looking over at her expectantly.

She rose on shaky knees and quickly headed to where the two officers waited. She instinctively grabbed the back of Flynn's winter coat as they stepped back out into the hall. Flynn hugged the wall as they made their way toward the rear exit.

The second attempt to leave the hotel was a success. Rhy was outside near an SUV, and he gestured for them to approach. "I'll follow you in my vehicle. Doug and Brady are staying here for now. They'll handle the questions from the local police."

"Good." Flynn took the key fob from Rhy's hand, then opened the back passenger door. "We'll want you in the back seat, Taylor. I need Cassidy to ride shotgun."

She nodded and climbed into the back.

Flynn shut the door and slid in behind the wheel. "Thanks, Rhy."

Rhy nodded and waited until the three of them were settled before jogging to his vehicle. Soon they were out on the road. She noticed Flynn eyeing the rearview mirror as they headed west. She turned to see several police vehicles converging on the City Central Hotel parking lot.

"That's another hotel that won't want our business anymore," Cassidy said with a wry smile.

Flynn grimaced. "I know. We already tried to cover our tracks by having the room secured by the DA's office through Rhy's brother-in-law Bax Scala. But we have used it as a safe house too many times before. I'm glad we're switching things up by using a rental under Doug's sister's name. The way this jerk keeps finding us is pissing me off."

Taylor tried to think positive. That their next stop

would be the one that would ensure her safety and Flynn's too.

But somehow, she didn't believe it. She stared out at the overcast gray November sky and prayed.

Please, Lord Jesus, keep us all safe in Your care. Amen.

FLYNN KEPT his eye on the rearview mirror. He watched for a tail, even though Rhy was directly behind them and likely doing the same thing.

He worked hard to take a circuitous route to Greenland, doubling back twice to make sure he didn't see anything suspicious.

There was nothing unusual in the area, but he couldn't relax. The nonstop gunfire was wearing on him. It bugged him that the shooter showed up at almost every single place they used as a safe house.

Proving they were anything but safe.

Which meant the guy who hired him must have significant resources at his disposal. After this most recent incident, he was more convinced than ever that included someone working against them from inside law enforcement.

SAC Donovan? One of the federal agents, Sally Fisk or Travis Goldberg? Both of them?

Someone else?

He had gone past the rental property twice when his phone rang. Seeing Rhy's name, he quickly answered. "What do you think? Is it safe?"

"Yeah, but let me go in first," Rhy said. "I'll walk around the exterior, then go inside. You stay back until I give the all clear."

"Understood." He'd rather be the one patrolling the perimeter but understood Rhy expected him to stick close to Taylor. Clearly, they should have done a sweep around the City Central Hotel. "We'll be waiting."

He drove through the park, pulling off to the side of the road at a deserted location. The cold chill in the air was keeping people out of the park, which was fine by him.

"What did they find in the parking structure?" Cassidy asked. "You mentioned a shell casing."

"Yes, Doug spotted a 9 mm shell casing. They'll send it to the lab for prints, not that I'm holding my breath." He shook his head. "It's not likely a professional would make a rookie mistake like leaving a fingerprint behind."

"You never know," Cassidy said. "If this is the work of one gunman, he's been awfully busy. He's bound to screw up one of these times."

"I don't know that he's alone," Taylor said from the back seat. "Whoever hired him must be feeling desperate. Maybe he's hired a second man to help Nickoli Yurgis."

"Anything is possible," he admitted. Taylor's comment reminded him that they already knew the identity of the gunman. Finding a fingerprint may not tell them anything they don't already know.

Unless there is a second player.

He still didn't know if Taylor's cousins Lyle and Jake were involved. He made a mental note to call Gabe later. Once they were settled in the rental house secured under Emily Sanders's name.

Was this a mistake? Yet if they didn't use Emily as a financial source, then who could they turn to? He hated feeling helpless.

He glanced at Taylor in the rearview mirror, then quickly looked away. Maybe if he hadn't been so distracted by kissing her, he'd have thought about searching the perimeter around the hotel.

That sort of mental lapse could not happen again. He needed to stay sharp and focused.

"What about food?" Cassidy asked, breaking into his thoughts. "We'll need to head out to buy supplies."

"Yeah, that's a good point. Cash only, though, at the local store." He shifted the car into gear and pulled back out onto the road that wound through Greenland Park. "I think we passed one just a few blocks away."

"I saw it," Cassidy said. "I'll head over once Rhy has cleared the place."

As if Rhy knew they were talking about him, Flynn's phone lit up with Rhy's name on the screen. "See anything suspicious?"

"Nope. The house to the north is dark without signs of anyone being home. There's an elderly couple in the house to the south. The property directly behind the rental has a car in the driveway, but I haven't seen anyone through the windows. Could be the occupant works a swing shift. The interior of the rental property is nice. I think this location will work out fine."

"Thanks." He appreciated Rhy's thorough assessment, and in theory, the location would work.

Yet he still intended to take precautions. There was still a slim chance they could be found if there was a leak within the FBI and that person made the connection between Doug and his half-sister's name on the agreement. Of course, that same person would need to have access to all local rental information in the first place, which seemed a stretch.

Maybe it was a good thing Doug and Brady had stayed

back at the City Central Hotel. Could federal phones be tracked? Was that how they'd been found?

He was driving himself crazy trying to pinpoint the issue. He left the park, went around the block, then pulled into the driveway of the rental property. Rhy had the garage door open, so Flynn took the hint. He parked inside and killed the engine.

"I think Cassidy should stay here with the two of you," Rhy said. "Unfortunately, Devon called to let me know she and Colleen are both sick with the flu, so I need to head home, at least for a little while."

"No problem," Cassidy quickly said. "I'll stick close."

"I'm sure we'll be fine," Flynn added. "But maybe tell your brother Brady and Doug to stay away. It occurred to me that their phones could have been tracked to the City Central Hotel."

"Good point." Rhy frowned. "Cass, turn your phone off and use one of the new disposable phones."

"Already done," Cassidy said. "I powered it down at the City Central."

"I'll be in touch," Rhy said as he turned away. "Stay safe."

Flynn led the way inside the rental, glancing around in surprise. Rhy was right; the place was nice. The furniture appeared comfortable, and the kitchen had been newly updated. There was a wide beautiful stone fireplace and a large stack of wood nearby.

"I wonder how much it costs to stay here," Taylor said. "It's pretty fancy for this neighborhood, don't you think?"

"Yeah, maybe, but nobody wants to rent something old and shabby. I'm sure the owners worked hard to make this place attractive to potential visitors." He crossed over to the kitchen and found a notepad and pen. "Taylor, work with

Cass to create a list of things you need from the grocery store. I'm going to take a few minutes to check the place out."

Cassidy looked as if she might argue. He gave her a pointed look that silently conveyed his wish that she stick close to Taylor rather than helping him out. He headed down the hallway to the bedrooms, searching each space thoroughly. While checking the closets, he was reminded of how this nightmare started. With Taylor and baby Max hiding out in the closet after the infant's parents were murdered in their beds.

After clearing the main level, he went down to the basement. The main portion was finished with carpet, painted walls, and more comfy furniture. He examined the utility area, looking behind the furnace, hot water heater, and water softener.

He took a moment to make sure the windows were locked, then returned to the main level. Taylor and Cassidy were finishing up the grocery list.

"Flynn, is there anything in particular you'd like?" Taylor asked.

"As long as you have coffee on the list, I'm good." He smiled. "I'm not picky as far as meals. I'll eat anything."

"Great. Then I'm heading out." Cassidy held out her hand, wiggling her fingers. "I need the key."

He dug the key fob for the SUV from his pocket and dropped it in the palm of her hand. Once she left, he turned toward the fireplace. He loved the scent of burning wood, and the house had a definite chill in the air.

He started a fire, using the kindling and paper that was clearly stacked nearby for that purpose. It didn't take long for the blaze to build, radiating heat into the room.

"I love watching the flames," Taylor said, curling up on

the sofa. There was a wistfulness in her tone that he'd not heard before. "Maybe I'm missing out by not having my own place. The fire makes it seem warm and cozy here."

"Yeah, it's always nice to have your own place." Glancing at her, he realized his mistake. Taylor was more beautiful than ever, her features soft in the glow of firelight. Dusk had fallen outside, and the intimacy of the setting was difficult to ignore.

He was treading on very dangerous ground.

Willing himself to stay away from her, he rose to his feet and looked around for something to do. The computer was likely still in Brady's car, not that he had any leads to dig into.

"Tell me about Lyle and Jake," he said, taking a seat in the chair kitty-corner from her. Far enough away, he thought to keep him from drawing her into his arms for another kiss. "I think you mentioned they hung out together but weren't that close to their brother Roman."

"I don't know Lyle and Jake at all." Her tone was testy. "I knew them as kids, Flynn. Not adults. I can't tell you their favorite colors or anything else that they were involved in. Other than airplanes," she added thoughtfully. "I seem to remember Lyle and Jake had several model airplanes in their bedroom."

Airplanes sounded like something a kid would find fascinating, but a hobby that could be left behind as an adult. He tried to come at her family from another angle. "When's the last time you saw their dad, your mom's brother?"

She sighed. "Probably a few years ago over Christmas. We honestly don't get together as often now that most of us are grown and gone."

That made sense, considering her younger sister and

brother were on opposite ends of the country. "Your siblings are the youngest of your cousins?"

"Yes." With a frown, she said, "I don't like thinking my family is involved in this. It makes me feel like I'm a suspect too."

"You're not a suspect, you're a witness." He attempted a smile. "Try to remember you're the innocent one in all of this. Even if your cousins are involved, that doesn't have anything to do with you."

"Easy for you to say." She wrinkled her nose. "It's not your family that's suspected of being involved in something illegal enough to kill over."

"Taylor, several members of the tactical team have discovered their family members were involved in crimes. Most recently, Roscoe's wife, Libby, was on the run from the cartel, and it turned out her father was involved. He ended up being shot and killed by Roscoe."

Her face paled. "Are you serious?"

"Yes. It was bad. But Libby and Roscoe are happily married now and have a baby. Everything worked out for them, and they'll work out for you too. Some people don't have the same moral code, or they're too easily swayed by the lure of easy money."

"Okay, okay." She threw up her hands and tipped her head back against the sofa cushion. "I get your point. I shouldn't feel responsible for my cousin's actions."

"Exactly." He resisted the urge to cross over to comfort her. "Everybody makes their own choices about how to live their lives."

"And you decided to become a cop." She pinned him with a serious gaze. "I can't imagine putting myself in harm's way each day."

He shook his head. "You can't think of it like that.

There are plenty of times we're able to diffuse a situation before it spirals out of control. I don't think about the danger unless we're called to the scene of a shooting, which thankfully isn't a daily event. I focus on the people I'm sworn to protect and serve."

She looked as if she wanted to say something, but his disposable phone rang interrupting the moment. Grateful for the distraction, he rose to his feet and moved into the kitchen. "Hey, Gabe, I thought you'd be home by now."

"I'm leaving here soon, but I stumbled across something interesting," Gabe said. "I found a second property owned by Investments, Inc. And it's a doozy. I'm not sure why we didn't find this before."

"What do you mean? What does the company own?"

"The bank itself," Gabe said with a hint of triumph in his voice. "The Brookland Bank property, the entire building, is fully owned by Investments, Inc. The corporation rents the space out to the bank."

"No way. Why haven't the feds found this connection?" he asked.

"Not sure, although I was about to reach out to Rhy next. I figure he can pass the intel along to his brother Brady and Ian, their tech expert."

"Yeah, okay. You may want to call Brady directly, though. Rhy went home because his wife and daughter are sick."

"I heard, you know how overprotective Rhy can be," Gabe said. "Devon is seven months pregnant, and he's worried about her. But there's one more thing I discovered. The Brookland Bank isn't the only company renting space. The entire top floor of the building houses another company. An investment firm called Financial Plus."

"Financial Plus? What does that mean?" Flynn asked.

"I don't know, but the first thing that popped into my mind was money laundering," Gabe said. "I'm no expert, but it's possible money is flowing from Financial Plus from allegedly people investing their money with them to the bank. Dirty money that is being siphoned through the bank to become clean."

"Good work, Gabe," he said, meaning it. "That is something that Brady, Doug, and Rhy need to know."

"I'll call Rhy next, then Brady if he doesn't answer," Gabe promised. "Later."

Flynn ended the call, his thoughts whirling. Money laundering appeared to be the motive behind the murders. But they were no closer to finding the person behind the company.

And he was once again suspicious of how well the feds were or weren't running the banking end of the investigation.

CHAPTER THIRTEEN

"What was that about?" Taylor eyed Flynn curiously after he ended his call.

"Looks like money might be the underlying motive for all this." He grimaced. "Gabe found another company that is owned by Investments, Inc. A firm called Financial Plus is also owned by the same company that owns the house on Peabody Lake. And that same company owns the building the bank is using."

No surprise about money being the motivator. She suspected that was mostly the reason for criminal activity. It hadn't been the reason for the danger shrouding Sienna and Bailey last month, but their situation was an aberration.

"I hope the rest of the pieces of the puzzle fall into place soon." She was glad Gabe had found something, but they weren't any closer to uncovering the person responsible.

"Me too." Flynn fell silent for a long moment, staring off into space. Despite being his usual supportive self, Taylor sensed Flynn was intent on keeping his distance from her. As if he regretted their kiss.

Oddly, she missed being in his arms. They were very

different people, but she was drawn to him in a way she'd never been drawn to anyone else. At least, not since her last relationship imploded.

Why wasn't Flynn involved in a relationship? He was a good-looking guy, strong, honorable, and courageously protective. Maybe not as classically handsome as Zeke and Rhy, but she found him very attractive.

An attraction she didn't want to believe was one-sided.

The sound of a car engine had Flynn leaping to his feet and striding to the door, his gun in hand. He'd moved faster than she could blink, a testament to his determination to keep her safe.

Maybe that was the problem, she thought with a sigh. *Maybe Flynn is only interested in keeping her safe. Nothing more.*

Sure, he'd kissed her. He was a guy after all. She had one serious boyfriend while in college, and she'd caught him cheating with her best friend. As she watched Flynn greet Cassidy at the door, helping with the groceries, she couldn't imagine him doing such a thing.

"It's snowing," Cassidy announced as she came inside. "Just flurries at this point, but the temperature must have dropped ten degrees since we got here."

"We'd better tune into the news," Flynn said. "Things have been happening so fast that I didn't even realize snow was possible."

"I listened to the radio in the car, and they mentioned we should expect snow flurries tonight. They aren't predicting a lot of precipitation, but you know how it goes." Cassidy flashed a smile. "They're wrong at least half the time. We could easily wake up tomorrow to twelve inches of snow."

Flynn shrugged as he unpacked groceries. "Doesn't much matter, as we're not going anywhere."

"We hope," Cassidy murmured, just loud enough for her to hear.

Taylor silently echoed that thought. She rose to peer out the window. The soft snowflakes were pretty, clinging to the tree branches and blades of grass. The first snow of the year was always the most beautiful with everything clean and white.

"I bought all the ingredients to make shrimp stir-fry for dinner," Cassidy said. "I like to cook, but after today, I thought it would be better to make something quick and easy."

"Great," Flynn said. "Quick and easy for me is fast food or pizza."

"As evidenced by the zillions of food wrappers strewn around your car," Taylor teased as she came into the kitchen.

Flynn winced at that but knew better than to argue since she was only speaking the truth. "Maybe, but shrimp stir-fry sounds delicious."

She stood at the counter. "What can I do to help?"

"Cut veggies," Cassidy said. "I can handle the rest."

When Flynn finished putting the groceries away, Taylor removed the veggies from the fridge and began chopping. She frowned when she noticed Flynn shrugging into his coat. "Where are you going?"

"To walk the property." His expression was serious. "I want to be sure the gunman doesn't sneak up to use us for target practice the way he did when we were at the City Central Hotel."

She tried to hide her concern as she nodded. "Okay. But come back soon."

"I have the disposable phone. Keep yours handy too." With that, he opened the back door and slipped into the cold.

"Hey, don't worry," Cassidy said, when she stood for a moment staring at the door. "Flynn knows what he's doing. Only the best of the best is given a position on Rhy's tactical team."

She smiled at that and resumed chopping veggies. "I get that, but it's hard to be the person responsible for placing cops like you in danger."

"That's our job," Cassidy said cheerfully. She cleaned the shrimp, then drizzled olive oil in a large frying pan.

"How well do you know Flynn?" Cassidy asked. She'd finished with the broccoli and started in on the cauliflower. "I mean, it's a little surprising he's still single."

Cassidy didn't say anything for a long minute, making Taylor fear she'd overstepped. She was about to say never mind when Cassidy answered. "I think Flynn has been hurt before, so he's probably guarding his heart." Cassidy swept the chopped broccoli together and dropped them into the frying pan. "You should ask Flynn about that, though."

"Of course. I didn't mean to pry." Okay, maybe she had meant to find out more about Flynn, but she didn't want Cassidy to feel as if she were breaking his confidence. She changed the subject. "That smells delicious."

"It's nothing fancy." Cassidy said, adding the chopped cauliflower to the mix. From there she began tossing other ingredients into the pan. Pea pods, water chestnuts, and spices like ginger and soy sauce.

Taylor finished with the veggies, then cleaned off the cutting board. Cassidy added the shrimp last, then began to stir.

Leaving Cassidy to finish dinner, she moved to the

closest window to check on Flynn. The only thing she saw were his footprints in the thin layer of snow.

Ten minutes later, he returned, stomping his feet to shake the snow loose and shrugging out of his coat. "Smells great."

"You're just in time. Dinner is ready," Cassidy announced.

"See anything unusual?" Taylor asked as Cassidy set the table.

"Nope. So far, so good." Flynn rubbed his hands together to warm them up. "Should have gotten gloves and a hat too."

"Let's eat." Cassidy waved a hand to the table. "Flynn, you can say grace."

It felt strange to sit down to a home-cooked meal. Once they'd all taken their seats, Flynn bowed his head. "Dear Lord, we thank You for this food and for the many ways You have kept us safe in Your care. Amen."

"Amen," she and Cassidy echoed.

"Dig in." Flynn reached for the bowl of rice with enthusiasm, making her wonder if he'd ever even tried to cook a meal for himself. Based on the plethora of fast-food wrappers in his car, she suspected not.

They ate in silence for several minutes. Flynn appeared lost in thought again, no doubt dwelling on the case. Then he glanced at her. "You and Cassidy pick which rooms you want to use. I plan on sleeping on the couch."

"That's fine." Just mentioning sleep made her yawn. Her brain was wired, but her body craved slumber.

When they finished eating, Flynn insisted on cleaning up. She and Cassidy picked their rooms, with Cassidy insisting she take the main bedroom. When she returned to the living room, she'd noticed Flynn was stretched out on the sofa with pillows and blankets he'd found in a closet somewhere and had fallen asleep.

She watched him for a moment, then turned to shut off the lights. She double-checked the door was locked, then went to bed.

But sleep didn't come easily, despite her fatigue.

Her thoughts whirled around Steve and Robin Miller, their son Max, and her cousin Roman. So much death and destruction over simple greed.

And when she finally drifted off an image flashed in her mind—dollar bills floating down onto their dead bodies like snowflakes falling from the sky.

FLYNN SLEPT like a rock for five hours before sitting upright with a jolt. He reached for his gun, glancing around to see what had awoken him.

Then he realized a log had fallen in the fire. Breathing out a sigh of relief, he rose and stretched, feeling better than he had before he'd gotten some sleep. He made the rounds, moving from one window to the next with no additional light other than that from the fire.

The snow was a blessing, as a layer of fresh powder covered everything in sight. The ground outside appeared undisturbed, and he could just barely make out the slight indents from his earlier footprints.

For the first time in what seemed like eons, he felt they were safe. Using Doug Bridge's sister's name to secure the rental seemed to have done the trick.

He crossed over to add more wood to the fire, then sank back down on the sofa. After setting his weapon aside, he scrubbed his hands over his face, wishing he could talk with

Rhy about the recent information Gabe had provided. And to have his boss check in with Detectives Klem and Irving to see what if anything they'd uncovered.

There was likely a BOLO out on Lyle and Jake Paulson. He hoped the two men would be found alive and not murdered like their older brother.

If this was about laundering dirty money, then why had the brothers' apartment been ransacked? What could the shooter have been searching for?

Maybe it was as simple as needing personal information on Taylor. So the gunman could find and silence her forever.

The hour was three in the morning, twenty-four hours since he'd rushed to the Miller residence to find Taylor. Twenty-four measly hours, and there had been so many attempts against her that he'd lost count.

He rose and paced, trying to come at the case from other angles. Money laundering was most often the result of illegal activities. Cash from selling drugs, gambling, and the like. But what had caused the guy in charge to have Steve and Robin murdered?

It was possible Steve hadn't realized his bank was being used to launder money. And that once he'd discovered what was going on, the guy in charge had eliminated Steve and his wife as threats.

But that didn't explain Roman Paulson's murder. And the more he thought about that, the more he felt like he was missing something. That there was some key to the case that he was overlooking.

He caught a flash of light through the window. A car? Or someone walking by?

Sweeping his gun off the end table, he moved swiftly toward the window overlooking the street. There were no houses directly across from there, only the wooded area of the park. He'd gone through that portion of Greenland Park earlier so that he knew what the terrain was like.

The snow covering the trees was still intact. Whatever he'd seen hadn't come from the woods. Most likely he'd caught a glimpse of a car passing by. They were in a regular neighborhood, and there were tire tracks in the snow on the street. More than one vehicle had been past in the time he'd slept.

Relaxing a bit, he watched for several more minutes to convince himself they were fine.

He stretched back out on the sofa, hoping to get a few more hours of sleep. No such luck. After changing cars so many times, they didn't have the laptop anymore. Maybe he could ask Rhy to send one over later that morning.

Just as he dozed off, he heard a thumping sound that had him jackknifing off the sofa. The sound had been too close for comfort.

Then he saw Taylor walking into the kitchen. She didn't seem to realize he was awake, as she grabbed a glass from the cupboard and filled it with water.

He waited until she was finished to make his presence known. "Hey, are you okay?"

She whirled to face him, her eyes wide. A moment later, she relaxed and nodded. "Sort of. I had a bad dream."

"Would you like to talk about it?"

She shook her head. "No. The dream itself didn't make any sense. I'm sure the stress of the day brought it on."

He stayed in the living room, hoping she'd head back to her room. She set her water glass aside, then walked toward him.

He almost took a hasty step back but caught himself. "Have a seat by the fire."

"Thanks." She didn't sit but stood holding her palms toward the flames. "It's hard to sleep not knowing what the day will bring."

"The good news is that we're safe here." He dropped back onto the sofa. "You still have time to get a few more hours of rest in."

"Yeah." She didn't look away from the fire for a full minute. Then she turned to face him. "Okay, maybe I do want to talk about part of my dream."

"Let's hear it." He was more than willing to be her sounding board.

"Don't laugh." She sat in the chair next to the couch. "I saw money raining down on the dead bodies of Steve, Robin, and Roman. I thought Max was dead, too, and ran toward him, but he wasn't. As I turned away, money still floating down on us from the sky, I saw Detective Irving standing off in the corner of the room, laughing. When I demanded she do something, that she try to help them, she just looked at me like I was pathetic and turned away, her shoulders still shaking with laughter."

He winced. "I know Irving is a hard case, but I'm sure she wouldn't really do that."

Taylor sighed. "Maybe not, but I just had the distinct impression that she couldn't have cared less about the dead people in the room."

He wasn't sure what to say to that. Detective Irving wasn't his favorite person, but he couldn't use Taylor's dream as a reason to accuse the woman of being dirty.

"I guess my subconscious knew I didn't like her and featured her in my dream as a bad guy," Taylor said. "Although that interview seems like weeks ago."

"I know." He smiled at her through the darkness. It wasn't easy to read her expression, but she looked wistful as she watched the fire. "Try not to worry. We have a lot of people working this case. I'm sure we'll learn something soon."

She nodded without saying anything more.

Strangely, the silence wasn't uncomfortable. It was almost as if he and Taylor had known each other for months rather than weeks.

She was still too beautiful for the likes of him, but he enjoyed watching her. As long as he didn't allow himself to get too close.

Close enough to be hurt when she left him once this nightmare was over.

When it appeared as if Taylor wasn't heading back to her room, he stood and moved to the window. He hadn't been able to get a full view of the entire yard since he hadn't gone into the two occupied bedrooms.

But now that Taylor was up and about, he could check the yard outside her windows.

"Did you do this all night?" she asked as he began what he'd started to think of as his window rounds.

"No, I managed to get some sleep." He flashed her a smile as he moved from the living room to the kitchen. "Just sit tight. This won't take long."

She shrugged and turned to continue watching the flames licking at the logs in the fire. He was glad he'd started it, even though he'd put a significant dent in the stack of wood that had been left inside. As he headed down the hall, he made a mental note to bring more wood in later.

Taylor's room smelled like her, but he forced himself to concentrate on the task at hand. The first window over-looked the neighbor's home, the one Rhy had mentioned belonged to an elderly couple. He watched for a moment but didn't catch any movement inside.

Moving to the next window, he could see a broader portion of the backyard. The woodpile was tucked in the left corner of the property.

Seeing nothing alarming, he turned away. Before he could take a step, he paused and looked back out the window. Something was off.

It took him a minute to notice that the dusting of snow on the woodpile was disturbed, as if someone had brushed it off. Frowning, he scanned the ground around the area but didn't see any footprints.

But this window and the other one from the kitchen only faced the front of the woodpile. Not the back.

Was someone hiding back there?

There was only one way to find out. He quickly turned and headed back to the kitchen to find his coat.

"What's wrong?" Taylor frowned when he shrugged into his coat and then reached for his gun. "Did you see something?"

He hesitated. "Probably nothing, but where's your phone? You should keep it handy."

"It's charging in my room." She stood and hurried to grab it.

He waited for her to return before reaching for the door handle.

"I don't think you're heading outside for nothing," she said in a low voice. "At least tell me what's wrong."

"Nothing is wrong. I just noticed the snow was missing along the top of the woodpile. Likely animals, like squirrels or raccoons." He wasn't sure what sort of wildlife roamed the area, but with the park across the street, he had to assume there were plenty of small game. "I just want to be sure."

"Okay." Taylor didn't look convinced. "If you're not back in ten minutes, I'm calling 911."

"Good. But you might want to wake up Cass first. She's armed and probably would want to back me up to keep you safe."

"Yeah, yeah." She waved him off. "Ten minutes."

He flashed a quick reassuring smile, then stepped out into the chilly night. It was cold enough to see his breath making puffs of steam in the air, and he stood for a moment to listen.

Silence.

Knowing he was making a big deal out of nothing, Flynn carefully crossed the lawn toward the woodpile. As he grew closer, he could see dozens of tiny paw prints in the snow from various animals.

But he could also see how a swath of snow along the top of the pile had been shoved to the side.

And not by a squirrel.

In his mind, he imagined a gloved hand making the movement. The hand slipping across the top of the pile as the person standing there lost his balance.

A chill that had nothing to do with the temperature washed over him. Bringing his weapon up in a ready stance, he crept closer. When he reached the woodpile, he used it for cover as he carefully looked behind it.

No one was there now, but they had been. The ground behind the neatly stacked wood was full of messy prints. Nothing clear enough to see, but several boot prints crossing each other as if the perp had stomped his feet to stay warm.

Someone had been there. And recently. It wasn't snowing now, and it was obvious there wasn't any fresh snow covering the messy prints.

Flynn slowly turned, sweeping his gaze across the

ground. Whoever had been out there hadn't crossed the lawn to get closer to the house.

So where was he?

A flash of movement from behind the garage caught his eye. He quickly turned in that direction in time to see a dark shape lift what appeared to be a gun.

"Stop! Police!" He hoped the guy would drop the gun, but he didn't. Even worse, the tip of the muzzle turned toward him. He was about to shout no when the guy fired at him.

Flynn dove to the ground, rolled over, and returned fire. He sent three rounds toward the perp; at least two of them appeared to strike the guy center mass.

The dark shape fell back against the garage, then slid to the ground. Flynn quickly raced forward, silently praying he hadn't killed him.

Partially because he'd never been forced to take a life, but even more so because they needed answers. He desperately wanted to know who had hired him to kill Taylor and why!

As he approached the fallen man, he noticed the guy was larger than he'd anticipated. Thicker around the middle than the stats he'd read on the mug shot of Nickoli Yurgis.

Kicking the gun away from the man's outstretched hand, Flynn lowered himself to a crouch beside the victim. With caution, in case the guy was going to make a move for the gun, he felt for a pulse.

To his surprise, he clearly felt the beat of the perp's heart beneath his fingertips. He was alive!

He was about to reach for his phone when Cassidy ran toward him, her weapon in hand. "What happened?"

"He shot at me, so I returned fire." He glanced up at her. "Did you tell Taylor to call 911?"

"Yes." Cassidy's attention was focused on the victim. "You have a pulse?"

"Yeah." He holstered his weapon and pulled off his coat. He balled it up and pressed it against the guy's chest where the bullets had struck him. "I'll hold pressure; you take his mask off."

"I don't see any blood," Cassidy said as she crouched beside him. "Are you sure you hit him? Maybe he was just grazed enough to be rendered unconscious."

"Positive." Although now that she mentioned it, he didn't see any blood either. The man groaned. "Hey, wake up! Are you hit? Wake up?"

The guy didn't respond.

Flynn felt along the front of the man's coat until his fingers found the holes in the coat made by the bullets he'd fired. But he also felt something else.

A thick layer of Kevlar.

"He's wearing a vest!" A sinking feeling hit hard as Flynn grabbed the lower edge of the man's black face mask, pulling it up and off in one smooth movement.

His jaw went slack when he recognized the shooter's face. *Taylor's dream was half right*, he thought grimly.

The bad guy wasn't Detective Irving, but the larger and more affable Detective Klem.

He'd shot a fellow cop.

CHAPTER FOURTEEN

The sound of gunfire had been all too familiar. Taylor had jumped to her feet and dialed 911 as she ran to wake Cassidy. Cassidy was already up and reaching for her weapon when Taylor burst into her room.

"Flynn's in trouble!" At that moment, the 911 operator answered the call. "Shots fired in Greenland, um, we're across the street from Greenland Park."

"Do you have the address?" the operator asked.

Cassidy must have heard because she rattled it off as she jammed her feet into her shoes. Taylor repeated it for the operator's benefit.

"Stay inside, ma'am, officers are on the way."

"There are officers here too. We're in danger so please hurry!" Taylor quickly ended the call, following Cassidy toward the back door.

"Stay inside," Cassidy said. "And keep away from the windows." With that, she'd slipped into the darkness.

Waiting was torture, and even though there were no more sounds of gunfire, Taylor couldn't relax. Couldn't stand not knowing what was going on or whether Flynn was all right or if he'd been shot.

Please, Lord Jesus protect Flynn and Cassidy!

The prayer helped, but as the silence outside stretched from five minutes to ten, her taut nerves felt as if they'd reached a breaking point.

Hearing the wail of sirens brought a sense of hope. Other officers would be there soon. And based on her recent experience over the past twenty-four hours, an ambulance would accompany them.

"Taylor?" Her heart squeezed in her chest when she heard Cassidy call her name. She ran to the back door and yanked it open, half expecting to see Flynn stretched out on the ground, bleeding into the snow.

But Flynn was standing near a different man who was lying on the ground. From here, she couldn't see any blood, but the way Flynn stood over him looking grim, she couldn't help but believe he'd been shot.

"I just wanted to let you know we're okay," Cassidy said gently. "The danger is over. I've cleared the yard. Stay inside where it's warm, this could take a while."

She nodded but sensed there was something wrong. "Flynn? Are you okay?"

He dragged his gaze from the fallen man who she realized now was handcuffed. "I'm not hurt. But you should know I shot Detective Klem. I identified myself as a cop and told him to drop his weapon, but he fired a round at me. I returned fire."

Detective Klem? The remnants of her dream flashed in her mind. Money falling onto the dead bodies of Steve, Robin, and Roman while Detective Irving stood off to the side watching with an evil smile.

Not Irving, but Klem.

Her stomach lurched, but she managed to fight back a wave of nausea. "I'm sorry you were put in this position. Is he dead?"

"No. He was wearing his vest." Flynn's voice was flat and emotionless, belying the anguish etched on his features. "He's out cold, though, so who knows? I can't say for sure he'll survive. Two slugs to the chest could have caused some heart damage."

She felt terrible for Flynn. Clearly this wasn't something he'd anticipated. And really, how could he? Detective Klem had appeared to be a nice, decent guy. He'd treated her well during her initial interview, and he'd been sweet toward Max too. She'd never gotten a hint of anything off about the guy.

Apparently, his easygoing attitude was nothing more than a lie.

The wind was cold, making her shiver, but she moved across the snowy ground toward him. Flynn abruptly lifted a hand to make her stop. "Don't," his voice was low and harsh. "You can't be out here. This is a crime scene."

She bit her lip, then reluctantly turned to head back into the rental house. This was a side of Flynn she hadn't seen before.

And she couldn't help but worry that this shooting had changed him forever.

Red and blue lights flashed through the window, indicating the Greenland police officer has arrived. She watched through the window as the officers joined Flynn and Cassidy. One officer used his flashlight to examine the ground, while the other spoke at length with the tactical team officers.

Flynn's fire had died down, but she didn't bother to add

more wood. No way would they be staying there for the next few days as planned.

Which made her wonder just how Detective Klem had found them.

As a cop, he had access to information, but to uncover the connection between Doug Bridges and his half sister and trace them here?

That seemed like a stretch. Unless there was another person also working for the bad guys within the FBI.

The theory was far from reassuring. They really couldn't trust anyone.

The door opened revealing Cassidy. "Hey, I wanted to be sure you're okay in here."

"I'm okay, but Flynn isn't." Taylor wasn't sure why she was confiding in Flynn's teammate.

"I know. He's taking it hard." Cassidy grimaced. "He didn't do anything wrong, but it's one thing to shoot a perp. It's another to shoot a cop."

"A dirty cop," Taylor swiftly corrected. "That's not the same thing."

"You don't have to convince me," Cassidy said. "Flynn knows he had to do it, but I think he's trying to figure out if Klem's being here was innocent somehow. That the detective wasn't involved in the money laundering or whatever is going on."

Taylor had never felt so helpless. Flynn was hurting, and she had no idea how to make him feel better. "Greenland is hardly in Klem's jurisdiction. I can't imagine he was here for some innocent reason. I can't even figure out how he found us."

"We're trying to uncover that angle too," Cassidy said with a sigh. "I just wanted you to know that we'll be tied up for a while yet. Our lieutenant, Joe Kingsley, is on his way as Rhy is still at home with his sick wife and daughter."

Taylor had met Joe once last month when things had heated up with Sienna and Bailey being in danger. Like the other members of the tactical team, he was a nice guy. "Okay. I'll make some coffee."

"We may end up being here for breakfast too," Cassidy said. "You're safe inside the house while the officers are here."

"I'll take care of that." Brewing coffee and making breakfast would give her something constructive to do. "Just keep an eye on Flynn, okay?"

Cassidy's expression softened. "I will. And Flynn is tougher than you think. He's taking this hard, but he'll bounce back. Especially once we find the evidence we need to link Klem to the gunman."

Cassidy spoke as if that connection was a foregone conclusion, and as Taylor set about making a pot of coffee, she hoped and prayed Cassidy was right.

That, for his sake, Flynn hadn't shot an innocent man.

FLYNN'S entire body was numb and not from the cold. He still couldn't believe he'd shot Detective Klem. Per protocol in an officer-involved shooting, he handed his weapon to the first Greenland officers on scene, instantly thinking of a way to get a replacement.

One thing was for sure, the danger surrounding Taylor was far from over.

"Other than the vest, Klem was dressed in street clothes," Cassidy said in a low voice as they watched the paramedics working on the fallen officer.

"That doesn't mean anything," Flynn said. Although he had found the dark clothing Klem wore from head to toe suspicious. Especially taking the black ski mask into consideration. "He's a detective, he wouldn't wear a uniform."

"Yes, but wearing black street clothes, hat, and mask while showing up at a safe house he shouldn't know about means you were in the right," Cassidy insisted. "Especially if you told him to drop his weapon."

"If?" He whirled on her. "I said I was a cop, told him to drop it, and he fired at me."

Cassidy lifted her hands. "Sorry, I didn't mean to make it sound as if I didn't believe you. I know you wouldn't just shoot without announcing yourself."

He blew out a long breath as he turned to watch Klem being lifted onto the gurney. "I pray he survives the shooting. We need answers as to who hired him. And how he's involved in this mess."

"He will." Cass sounded confident. "The bullets didn't pierce his chest, bone, or muscle. He's badly bruised and having some heart issues, but there's no reason to suspect he'll die from being shot in the chest."

It was still difficult to comprehend he'd shot a fellow officer. A likely dirty and corrupt officer, but a fellow brother in blue just the same.

Jina and her husband, Cole, had interacted with Klem and Irving two months ago. They hadn't gotten any hint of Klem being dirty. Irving had been her usual pain-in-the-behind self, especially with Jina.

But everyone had gotten along well with Klem.

"Looks like they found a shell casing," Cassidy said, breaking into his thoughts. "That reinforces your story that he fired at you."

He wanted to shout at the top of his lungs that it wasn't

a story, but he managed to bite his tongue. Cassidy wasn't pointing out anything he didn't already know. He'd shown the first officers on scene where he'd been standing when Klem had fired. How he'd ducked and rolled to return fire. The disturbed snow on the ground had been obvious.

The shell casing would help too. And he didn't doubt that the crime scene techs would be able to verify that Klem's weapon had been fired recently. The officers on scene had been smart enough to place Klem's gloves in an evidence bag to be tested for gunshot residue. They'd snagged the ski mask too.

Yet Flynn knew that a good lawyer could easily claim Klem was innocent. That he'd dressed for the cold and hadn't known Flynn was a cop. The only thing that worked in Flynn's favor was the fact that Greenland was outside of Klem's jurisdiction and that the detective shouldn't have known about their being at the rental property in the first place.

It bothered him that Klem had found them. He'd felt certain the leak was within the FBI, not the local police.

Could it be both? He hated to believe it, but at this point, he wasn't ruling anything out.

Everyone was a suspect until he was convinced other-wise. Except for his tactical team family. And the Finnegans, including Doug Bridges as well.

If not for Doug nearly being shot by the gunman outside the City Central Hotel, Flynn would be tempted to lump him in with the pile of suspects. But he knew from Rhy and others within their team, like Roscoe, that Bridges had helped cover their backs.

As Taylor was handing out cups of coffee, Lieutenant Kingsley arrived. Joe raked his gaze over him. "Are you okay?"

"Peachy." Flynn took a sip of the steaming brew, hoping to absorb some of the warmth. "We need to get Taylor out of here."

"Soon," Joe promised. "Right now, we have more than enough officers on scene to keep her safe."

While true, the swarm of officers didn't make Flynn feel any better. He was about to argue, when Taylor said, "Breakfast will be ready in ten."

"You and Cassidy go inside," Joe said. "I'll stick around out here for a bit."

Since the coffee wasn't working to warm him up, Flynn took his boss's advice. He turned and led the way inside, then paused to glance back at Joe. "I need a backup weapon. I had to give mine to the local cops."

"Understood," Joe said with a nod. "I'll get one from the gun case at Rhy's place. He won't mind."

The close proximity of Greenland to Brookland reminded him of Detective Klem and the way the guy had crumpled to the ground from the force of his bullets. Which gave him another thought. "Detective Irving needs to be relieved of her duties until we know for sure she's not working with Klem. Especially since we have no idea how Klem figured out we were here. I'm concerned someone higher up in the Brookland PD is also involved. Not to mention there could still be someone inside the FBI working for the bad guys."

Joe winced, then nodded. "Yeah, okay. I'll take care of it."

Flynn finally walked inside the rental. He stood in the kitchen for a moment, wondering why he didn't feel warm yet.

Maybe he'd never be warm again.

"Here, let me refill that for you." Taylor took his half-empty mug and topped it off with fresh coffee. "You look chilled."

That was an understatement. He hadn't felt this cold after he and Taylor had escaped the sinking boat in Peabody Lake. As he sipped his coffee, he noticed the fire in the fireplace was nearly burned out. Setting the cup aside, he strode over to revive it.

When he finished adding wood and stoking the fire, he stared into the leaping flames, wondering how they were going to find a place for Taylor that would keep her safe and secure for the duration of this investigation.

Then again, maybe it wasn't a matter of where, but a matter of how many officers they had posted around her. As Joe had mentioned, they were safe here because of the numerous officers on scene.

Enough to scare off one lone gunman.

And where was Nickoli Yurgis anyway? Flynn had assumed the masked gunman was Yurgis since Taylor had seen him after he'd murdered the Millers. Tearing off the mask to find Klem lying there had been an unwelcome surprise. Why had the detective been tasked with coming to their safe house tonight?

Or more accurately, this morning?

Too many questions without answers.

"Flynn, are you ready to eat breakfast?"

Taylor's voice had him turning to face her. Suddenly the scent of bacon and eggs made his stomach growl. He wasn't sure how, but the fire had reached deep within to warm his chilled soul.

Maybe God was trying to let him know everything was okay.

"Thanks, Taylor." He rose to his feet and crossed the

room. From the anxious expression in her blue eyes, he decided she'd been worried about him.

As if he was the one in danger.

"I'd like to say grace," Taylor said as they took their seats. It seemed strange to be sitting and eating while officers roamed the crime scene outside. But they were stuck in the house until they'd gathered every scrap of evidence there was to be found and cleared the area.

"Sure." He was surprised when she took his hand beneath the table.

"Dear Lord Jesus, we thank You for this food we are about to eat. We also thank You for keeping us all safe in Your care. Especially Flynn. Amen."

"Amen," Cassidy said.

His throat was thick with emotion, but he managed to croak out a response. "Amen."

Taylor held his hand for a long moment before releasing it. He was touched by her concern, even if he wasn't sure he deserved it. He picked up his fork and dug into the scrambled eggs, bacon, and toast.

"Tastes great," Cassidy said.

"Breakfast is easy." Taylor smiled and gestured to the pan in the center of the table. "I made plenty if any of the officers outside are hungry and allowed to eat."

"Usually not while on duty." He took a bite of his toast. "The good news is that they didn't arrest me."

Taylor's eyes widened in horror. "Is that a possibility?"

Cass sent him an exasperated glance. "I don't think you need to worry about that. Once we explained about the danger to you, and the number of murders that have already taken place, the local cops believed our version of events. Joe will coordinate with their leadership to smooth things over."

Plagued by a sense of urgency, Flynn ate quickly. He didn't want to stick around any longer than necessary, especially if the cops outside were about finished processing the scene of the crime.

His disposable phone rang. Recognizing Rhy's number, he answered. "Hey, Rhy."

"Are you okay? What's this about you shooting Klem?" Rhy asked.

Suppressing a sigh, Flynn filled him in on the recent events. "I assume Joe called to let you know I need a weapon."

"Yeah, he left a message. I called you directly because I was concerned." Rhy's voice sounded heavy with regret. "I think I may have blown it with Klem."

The admission shocked him. "What do you mean?"

"It's my fault," Rhy said. "I ran into Klem last night when I got home. I didn't think much about his being at my place, waiting to update me on the investigation. He told me they had a line on Lyle and Jake and were heading to one of their friends' houses to see if they could find him."

Flynn caught Cassidy's eye, then glanced at Taylor. Both were listening to his side of the conversation. "Okay, so Klem was at your place last night, and you spoke to him. How much did you tell him about where we were staying?"

Cass grimaced as Taylor gasped.

"I didn't give him your address or anything, but I mentioned you guys were safe in Greenland." Rhy muttered something under his breath, then added, "I was sidetracked by Devon and Colleen being sick, especially since Devon began having some contractions despite not being due for two months. But that's no excuse. I shouldn't have mentioned Greenland. I'm sorry."

"Telling Klem we were staying in Greenland isn't the same as giving him an address," Flynn said thoughtfully. "But that may have allowed him to narrow it down."

"I feel terrible, and I've already put a call in with the Brookland PD Chief of Police," Rhy said. "I want the department to verify Klem's partner, Irving, isn't involved. And I need them to investigate Klem's actions from their end too."

"Good." He tried to smile reassuringly at both Cassidy and Taylor. He didn't feel that much better about shooting Klem, but knowing Rhy had made the slip was oddly reassuring.

Eleven months ago, when Steele and Harper had been in danger Flynn had slipped up by giving key information about a safe house location to a dirty ATF agent. He'd carried the heavy yoke of guilt for months afterward, despite Rhy, Steele, and the others reassuring him that it could have happened to anyone.

Now that a similar slip had happened to Rhy, he guessed they were right about that. What had Taylor said? They were all human and bound to make mistakes.

Yet it still didn't explain how Klem had found the connection to Doug Bridges's sister, Emily Sanders, to find their exact address.

Process of elimination? Had Klem gone to all the rental properties listed in Greenland? How many could there be? Probably not that many. And if not for the lack of snow on the woodpile, Flynn might not have gone out to investigate.

God certainly had watched over them tonight.

"I hope you can forgive me," Rhy said. "I feel awful that I let you down."

"You've always been supportive, so that's not even an

issue. Besides, you forgave me when I goofed earlier this year," Flynn said. "In a way, it helps to know that the feds may not be involved."

"We don't trust anyone outside the family and Doug Bridges," Rhy said. "I'll work with Joe to get Taylor to the safe house. I've given the order to move the current occupants out ASAP to free it up for you."

The news brought a wave of relief. At least the safe house had bullet-proof windows. And it wasn't in Greenland either. With Klem in the hospital and Irving soon to be benched, they didn't have to worry about anyone inside the law enforcement community finding them there. Police precincts didn't share safe houses, and his being forced to shoot a dirty cop reinforced the wisdom of that policy.

"Stay put for now," Rhy said. "I'll let Joe know when you're cleared to move to the safe house."

That gave him pause. "I don't want to stay here once the officers outside disperse. We don't know for sure Klem didn't tell Irving his plans to come here. And we still don't know where Nickoli Yurgis is either."

"I'll convince the Greenland police to keep their officers there for as long as it takes," Rhy said. "Don't worry about that."

"Okay. Thanks. Keep us posted on the timeline."

"Will do." Rhy ended the call.

"Wow, I can't believe Rhy accidentally gave away our location," Cassidy said as they finished eating. "He is always so on top of things."

"Devon had contractions, so I can understand why he was distracted." He glanced at Taylor, thinking about how he'd allowed his attraction to her distract him too.

No more, he silently vowed.

"If we're sticking around for a while, I wouldn't mind

taking a shower," Taylor said, rising to her feet and carrying her dirty dishes to the sink. "I'll clean up after I'm finished."

"I'll do it," Cassidy offered.

"I'll help." Flynn chewed the last slice of bacon as he carried his plate to the sink. He was glad Taylor hadn't seen his place with the dirty dishes stacked in the sink. He'd have to do better on that front too.

Not that he expected to see Taylor again once this was over.

He thrust his hands into the hot, soapy water to force himself to think about something, anything other than his conflicted feelings toward Taylor.

"What do you think? Is Irving also involved?" Cass asked as she picked up the towel to dry.

"Don't know. She's easy to dislike, but that's not proof of wrongdoing."

"Yeah, I get the impression Irving has had a tough life," Cassidy said. "Then again, so did Jina and Raelyn and they're not soured on life."

"Because of the team," Flynn said. "I mean, think about it. We are all very supportive of each other. That level of camaraderie isn't common in all police departments."

"True," Cassidy agreed. They washed and dried dishes for the next few minutes. Then he looked out the window, relieved to see there were four cops milling about outside.

The crime scene techs were just finishing up as well. They were easy to spot in their head-to-toe water-resistant gear. They looked like puffy dolls.

He made another pot of coffee, trying not to glance at his watch. Taylor seemed to be taking a long time. Was she crying again? Feeling overwhelmed by everything that had happened?

Setting his coffee aside, he moved down the hall. His

hand went to his hip before he remembered he didn't have his gun.

A muffled thump made his heart jump in his chest. He lunged forward to grab the door handle, yanking it open.

Then he froze when he saw a man dressed in water-resistant gear holding Taylor at gunpoint.

CHAPTER FIFTEEN

When Taylor had finished getting dressed in the bathroom, she'd stepped into the room in time to see a man wearing cream-colored head-to-toe protective gear, including face mask and goggles, coming in through the window. She must not have heard the noise over the sound of the shower and blow-dryer.

Before she could scream, he leveled the gun at her as he finished climbing through the opening. "Don't say a word."

She'd instinctively backed up, slamming into the door behind her. She assumed the man standing before her was Nickoli Yurgis, but she couldn't tell because of the face covering. She tried to steady herself, knowing she needed to buy time. To find a way to stay alive. "Who are you? What do you want?"

Before the gunman could respond, her bedroom door burst open, revealing Flynn. Seeing Flynn's empty hands, Taylor screamed, "No!" at the top of her lungs and lunged toward the gunman just as he moved the muzzle of his weapon toward Flynn.

Two sharp reports reverberated through the small

space. Taylor half expected to feel the impact of a bullet as her momentum carried her forward, but surprisingly, it was the gunman who stumbled backward, crumpling to the floor in a heap.

Flynn moved quickly across the room with Cassidy behind him. Taylor had fallen half on top of the gunman and was trying to scramble out of the way in case he turned the weapon on her.

But he didn't get the chance. Even though she hadn't seen the gunman move, Cassidy fired two more rounds into his body.

"Taylor!" Flynn reached for her. "Are you hurt?"

"I don't think so." She sagged against Flynn, looking down at herself as if to make sure she hadn't been hit by a bullet. Everything had happened so fast she wasn't sure her brain had processed the event. Two shots had been fired. "What about you?"

"I'm fine," Flynn said. "His shot went high because you threw yourself at him."

"He's no longer a threat," Cassidy said. Her gaze was somber as she turned to face them. "Are you both okay?"

"How did you know he was in here?" Taylor asked. She was surprised that Cassidy had been able to shoot past Flynn in the narrow space. "I didn't even know until I came out of the bathroom."

"I heard a thumping sound." Flynn clutched her close, and she could feel the thundering beat of his heart beneath her ear. "I just knew you were in trouble."

"And when I saw you jumping toward the bedroom, I followed since I knew you weren't armed," Cassidy said. She shook her head. "Foolish move, Flynn. However, I am glad you moved to the side in time to give me a clean line of sight to the perp."

"I was hoping you'd hit him," Flynn admitted. "And I was halfway to the door before I remembered I didn't have my gun."

"Thankfully, Taylor helped to knock him off guard." Cassidy nodded at her. "Nice work."

She didn't point out that she hadn't done it on purpose. Her only thought was to prevent the intruder from killing Flynn. In that moment, she'd realized how much she loved him.

"You shouldn't have done that," Flynn scolded. "You could have gotten hurt when Cassidy took the shot."

She shrugged. Thankfully, Cassidy was an expert marksman. "Who is he?" She stared at the fallen man, noticing with horror that the pale Tyvek suit had a pool of blood forming in the center of his chest. If the gunman was Nickoli Yurgis, he wouldn't be killing anyone ever again.

Cassidy removed the fallen man's face mask. When Taylor saw the man's face, she gasped. "That's Lyle. My cousin Lyle!"

"I'll call Joe," Flynn said. "Jake might be dressed just like this and waiting for us outside!"

Instantly, Cassidy moved toward her and Flynn, taking up a protective stance as she faced the open window.

Not open, she abruptly realized. And not broken either. The glass had been cut and removed. How had Lyle accomplished that without anyone noticing? Probably his wearing the Tyvek suit meant no one paid him much attention.

"Joe? Cass shot Lyle Paulson who got inside the house dressed as a crime scene tech," Flynn said curtly. "His brother Jake could be outside wearing the exact disguise."

"Got it, stay put." As Taylor was still pressed against Flynn, it was easy to hear Joe's response.

Almost instantly, a series of shouts could be heard from

the backyard. Cassidy moved toward the window, staying off to the side to avoid being a target. Then she glanced over with a wry grin. "Looks like they found him." Her eyes gleamed with satisfaction. "He's down on the ground with several weapons pointed at him."

"Good," Flynn responded. "That accounts for three suspects; however, we are still missing any information on the whereabouts of Nickoli Yurgis and the mastermind who hired them."

The man who'd almost killed her was not Nickoli but her cousin. Her own relative had come into the house with the intent to eliminate her. How could Lyle do such a thing? She felt as if she'd been kicked in the chest.

Then she wondered if one brother, Lyle or Jake, had killed their oldest brother, Roman, as well. And if Lyle and Jake were involved, why had their place been searched? That part didn't make any sense.

Most of this nightmare didn't make sense. They needed to understand why the Millers had been murdered. Would they ever know the truth? She was beginning to fear that their questions would forever remain unanswered.

"I think it's safe to go to the kitchen," Cassidy said. "Guess I'll be giving up my service weapon now too."

"Not until we know we're safe," Flynn said sharply. "I'm angry with myself for not insisting on keeping mine."

"Yeah, not very smart of you to rush into danger unarmed," Cassidy teased. Then her expression turned somber. "I guess we know now that Detective Klem told Lyle and Jake Paulson about this place."

"Yeah, their showing up like this, dressed as crime scene techs, screams of a backup plan. Almost as if Klem had known it wasn't likely that he'd succeed," Flynn said.

That possibility hadn't occurred to her. Taylor moved

into the kitchen, sinking into the closest chair. Flynn stayed beside her, as did Cassidy. The interior of the house was getting colder by the minute, so Flynn quickly crossed the room to toss more logs into the fire.

As Flynn returned to her side, the back door opened, revealing a grim-faced Joe Kingsley. "We've arrested Jake, but he's not talking."

Flynn scowled. "That's fine. We know what he and Lyle had planned."

"We may believe they're involved in this up to their eyeballs, but the truth is that our case against Jake isn't great," Joe said. "We have him for impersonating a crime scene tech, carrying a firearm, and conspiracy to commit murder. But at this point, Lyle is dead, and Klem is in the hospital, so it's his word against theirs. He's claiming he's innocent, that he had no intention of killing anyone and will only talk to his lawyer."

Joe's comments washed over Taylor like ice water. "But he and Lyle do everything together. There's no way Lyle was involved in this without Jake's help and support."

"Your testimony to that effect will help," Joe admitted. "But we'll still need more proof to make sure Jake goes away for the rest of his life."

"We'll just have to keep working the case until we find the evidence we need," Flynn said flatly. "Because I agree with Taylor, there's no way he's not involved."

"I hear you." Joe raked a hand over his hair. "More Greenland cops are on their way back here. We're going to keep the place surrounded until we can get you and Taylor transferred to the safe house."

"Wait, we're still going?" She glanced from Flynn to Joe and then Cassidy. "I don't understand. We know Klem has been taken out of the picture. Surely, we're safe now."

There was a long silence as the three cops exchanged sympathetic glances.

"We're going to the safe house until we know the man in charge," Flynn finally said. "Until we have that piece of the puzzle, we're not lowering our guard."

Joe's phone rang. He pulled it from his pocket and answered. "Hey, Rhy. I'm putting you on speaker because things have been happening here."

There was a pause before she heard Rhy's voice. "I just heard from Cole Roberts; you might remember he's a Peabody detective. A dead body was pulled from Peabody Lake and has been positively identified as our Russian Mafia thug, Nickoli Yurgis. Looks like he was shot in the head, then tossed in the water."

"Well, that's not good," Cassidy muttered.

Flynn looked upset, as did Joe. And she understood why. If they couldn't convince her cousin Jake to talk, they'd never learn who was behind all these murders.

And it was entirely possible she'd never be safe again.

"WE NEED to huddle at the safe house," Flynn said. "Brady and Doug too. There has to be a way to figure out who hired Yurgis and the Paulson brothers. To find whoever planned these murders and why."

"I like the huddle idea," Rhy said. "Unfortunately, I'm taking Devon to the hospital while Elly watches over Colleen. She's dehydrated and her OB doc recommended she be seen to get IV fluids. They think her dehydration is causing the contractions. The flu season is apparently pretty bad this year."

"We'll pray for Devon," Cassidy said, her expression

full of concern. "Of course, you should stay focused on your family. Joe is here, and we'll get some of the other members of the team to head out too. I believe that by working together we'll figure this out."

"I feel bad I can't help, but I'll call Brady and make sure he and Doug meet up with you. Stay put until then."

Flynn wanted to argue that staying put had almost gotten Taylor killed but held back. None of this was Rhy's fault. Nobody anticipated that Klem might be on the take. Thinking along those lines gave him an idea. "Thanks, Rhy. We'll take it from here." He disconnected the call, then said, "We need someone to interrogate Klem the moment he's able to talk. And we should reach out to the Paulson siblings' parents." He turned to look at Taylor. "What is the first names of your aunt and uncle?"

"I'm sure my mom's brother isn't involved," Taylor protested. "He's not rich and wouldn't have money to invest, especially after the divorce." When he simply waited, she sighed. "Donald Paulson. Don and Gail Paulson. I'm not sure Gail kept the last name, though. She might be under Gail Lee."

"I'll talk to Gabe, maybe he can dig into their backgrounds too," Joe said.

It was frustrating to stand there, waiting for the rest of the cavalry to show up. Flynn tried not to stare at his watch as he wondered how long it would take.

"Hey, I have a guy out here who wants to talk to whoever is in charge," one of the cops said, poking his head through the doorway. "Claims to have information on the murders?"

Joe was closest to the door and glanced behind the officer. Flynn stepped forward, a rush of adrenaline hitting hard. "I'll talk to him."

"Negative. He says he'll only talk to his niece, Taylor Templeton."

"Uncle Don is out there?" Taylor rushed toward the door before he could stop her. Thankfully, Joe snagged her arm before she could get all the way outside.

"Taylor! What happened to Lyle and Jake?" The man's voice sounded agonized, as if he already suspected the worst. That his two sons had been murdered the same way his oldest had been.

"Uncle Don, Lyle tried to kill me!" Taylor leaned past Joe, craning her neck to see better. Joe abruptly yanked Taylor down at the same moment a crack of gunfire rang out.

"Gun, gun!" someone shouted.

Flynn rushed to Taylor, pulling her back from the doorway. Sounds of a scuffle broke out, then there was nothing but silence.

"We have her." The voice sounded strained. "She wounded him, though."

She? Flynn glanced down at Taylor who looked horrified as the news sank in. Taylor surged to her feet. He caught her in his arms, holding her close.

"I want to see him. My uncle Don. I want to see him!" Her blue eyes were bright with tears.

"The area isn't secure," Flynn protested. Talk about a giant understatement. First Klem found them, then the Paulson brothers, now Taylor's uncle Don and possibly her aunt? Who else could the woman be out there?

"What's going on?" Flynn recognized Brady's voice. Feeling slightly better now that reinforcements had arrived, he relaxed his grip on Taylor. But instead of heading outside, she turned into his arms, burying her head against his chest.

"Brady? Is Doug with you?" Flynn asked.

"Yeah. How on earth did Irving get out here?" Bridges asked. "I thought she was supposed to be taken into custody?"

Irving? Not Gail Lee? He glanced at Taylor in confusion. "Are you sure the woman is Irving? We were concerned about a person by the name of Gail Lee. Gail Lee, formerly Gail Paulson. She used to be married to Don Paulson and her sons are Roman, Lyle, and Jake."

There was a brief pause, before Doug said, "This woman's ID is for a Gail Lee. But she looks very similar to Detective Irving."

Taylor's mouth dropped open. "I totally forgot that Gail has a twin sister! I haven't seen her in so long I didn't recognize Detective Irving as being related to the family."

One of the puzzle pieces fell into place. It seemed as if Gail had gotten her sons involved in whatever crime was being committed. And she was also Irving's twin sister. Which probably meant Irving was dirty too.

Did that mean Klem was innocent?

Flynn didn't want to believe he'd shot an innocent man, even if the guy had fired at him first. His thoughts whirled as he comforted Taylor. Her family had been far more involved in this than any of them had realized.

And they still didn't know who was in charge of the scheme.

As if on cue, Joe's phone rang. He answered without putting the call on speaker. "Gabe, what do you have for us?"

Flynn found himself praying that Klem was dirty. That shooting the detective would be justified. At least in the eyes of the law.

On a personal level, he knew that firing at Klem would

stick with him for a long time. Cops were put in positions where they had no choice but to take down bad guys. It wouldn't be his first or his last.

But he still felt guilty and prayed Klem would survive.

"Thanks, Gabe, you have perfect timing. We have Gail Lee in custody. I'll let the others know." Joe lowered his phone, a smile breaking across his features. "Gabe cracked the case. He finally identified the owners of Investments, Inc. A guy by the name of Allen Irving. Who, as you know, is married to Detective Irene Irving."

"You're kidding. Irving's husband is the brains behind this?" Flynn couldn't believe it.

"Yep. And he dragged his wife, sister-in-law, and likely Klem into the snare, likely promising them easy money," Joe confirmed. "Although we don't have everything we need yet, we still have to connect Allen Irving to Nickoli Yurgis and to whatever money issues were going down at the bank. Hopefully, the feds will do their part on the banking end of things. Gabe will reach out to Ian with what he's found. Based on the link between Financial Plus and Investments, Inc., I think a warrant will be issued for Allen Irving's arrest. And his wife's arrest, too, if she's not already in custody," Joe added.

"Does that mean it's over? Like for good this time?" Taylor asked. She looked a little shell-shocked, but she wasn't crying anymore.

"Yes, but we'll move you to the safe house anyway until we know for sure," Joe said.

"I'll stay with you for as long as it takes," Flynn said reassuringly. He wanted to add that he'd be there forever if she'd let him.

But they'd never broached the subject of what they'd do when this was over. She was the pretty girl who under normal circumstances wouldn't look at him twice. This—whatever they had between them—was based on fear and danger. Emotions that would fade over time.

"Thank you, Flynn." She reached up to cup his cheek with her hand. "I am very grateful to have your support."

He felt his ears turn red with embarrassment. Suddenly Joe and Cassidy disappeared outside, leaving him and Taylor alone.

"I know you've been through a lot," he said. "I'm happy to help you get settled once this is over."

"I would like that," she murmured. "In fact, I think I'd like to stay with you for a while." She flushed, then added, "If you'll let me."

"I, uh, sure." Her comment knocked him off balance. "You can stay with me as long as it takes."

She tilted her head to the side. "As long as it takes for what?"

"Um." He had no idea how to answer. "For as long as you need. Things have happened fast, but I don't think you should make any snap decisions about your future. It might be smart to take some time to think about what you want to do."

She nodded thoughtfully, searching his gaze for a minute. "What I really want, Flynn, is to spend more time with you."

His heart soared, but his brain was already tampering down his excitement. "That's sweet, but being forced together like this isn't natural. What I mean is, I'm sure you'll want to move on with your life once you've recovered from this."

"You're right; this has been a bit stressful," she said with a frown. "But you're not understanding me. I care about you. When I thought Lyle was going to shoot you, I wanted to claw his eyes out. This isn't just forced proximity talking. This is me getting to know you again. And wanting more."

More? Hope warred with logic. "Come on, Taylor. I know I'm not your type."

Now her eyes flashed with anger. "What do you know about my type? I care about men who have traits like honor, integrity, courage, and who are known to be trustworthy. The trust part is most important since I know what it's like to be cheated on."

He was shocked by that. "Who in their right mind would cheat on you?"

Her anger relaxed into a smile. "Ah, Flynn. Don't you see? Other than maybe your tendency to be a slob, you're exactly my type."

It was nice to hear, even if he didn't really believe it. He was sure her feelings were honorable, too, but once the danger was over, things would change. Day-to-day life would reveal potential flaws in their relationship.

And he wouldn't want to hold her back.

"I'm getting the sense you don't think I know how I feel about you. That those feelings will change at some point." She looked a bit exasperated. "Do you remember what I said last month shortly after we first met?"

He remembered with painful clarity. "Yes. You were angry with me and Zeke and told us we would never be the hero of your story."

She nodded. "Yep, except that I lied. As I continued to write my story, you became the hero. I described him to match you. He acted exactly the way you've been responding to the threats of danger we faced. He's tough, sweet, brave, and supportive in every way. My hero is you, Flynn."

"Me?" Shock rippled through him. Was she serious? "I don't understand."

Now she shook her head, clearly annoyed. "What's not to understand? For the last time, I care about you. I think I'm falling in love with you."

Since he'd completely run out of words to say, he decided to let his feelings speak for him. He drew her close and kissed her.

Taylor melted against him, wrapping her arms around his neck and pulling him closer as she returned his kiss. And slowly it dawned on him that maybe she was being truthful.

Because no woman had ever kissed him like that.

"Flynn? Oh, sorry." The cheerful tone in Steele's tone belied his apology. As did the goofy grin on his teammate's face. "Hey, if you're not too busy, Brady wants me to escort you to the safe house as the feds head out to make the arrests."

"We are busy," Taylor complained. "I don't know who you are but go away."

Flynn found himself grinning back as Steele laughed.

"Okay, okay. I'll give you guys a few minutes," Steele said between chuckles. "But don't take too long or I'll send Joe in."

"Thanks. We'll be out soon." Flynn wasn't in any hurry to let Taylor go, but he knew they couldn't stay there much longer either. Despite the heat they'd generated between them, the air held a distinct chill.

The fire in the fireplace had burned down to hot coals again.

"Look, Flynn, I don't mean to be pushy, but please tell me that my feelings aren't one-sided." A flicker of uncertainty darkened her eyes. "That I'm not the only one who wants to see where a relationship might take us."

"I love you. I may not be a writer with pretty words, but I fell in love with you a while ago, probably the first time we met." He brushed a light kiss over her mouth. "Based on your annoyance with me, I figured you didn't feel the same way. The other night when you texted me about seeing the gunman, I was terrified I'd never get the chance to tell you how much I loved you."

"Really?" She stared up at him in surprise. "You really love me?"

That she could doubt his feelings made him realize they were both being idiots about this. Yes, they'd been thrown together in difficult circumstances, but that didn't mean their feelings weren't real.

That their love wouldn't last.

"Yes, I really love you, Taylor. I would love for you to stay with me once we're released from the safe house. You use my guest bedroom; I would never take advantage of the situation." He managed a smile. "Even more importantly, I'll support you in whatever you decide to do. Whether you go back to being a nanny, teaching, writing, or whatever brings you happiness. I'm there for you."

"Oh, Flynn." She drew him in for another kiss. After a long moment, she said, "I want to support you too. I'm sure this had been difficult, especially after what happened with Detective Klem. I'm here if you want to talk about it. Or anything else for that matter."

"You're amazing," he whispered.

"So are you." She smiled. "I'm so blessed that God brought you into my life."

Flynn knew they were blessed. Not just because they'd survived, but because God's love shone down on them.

This moment right now was what true love was all about.

EPILOGUE

Thanksgiving Day . . .

Taylor was a little nervous being invited to Thanksgiving with some of Flynn's teammates. Rhy had insisted on having several of them come to the homestead, a term he used to describe his house. Not everyone could be there, Brock and his wife, Liana, were out of town, and Zeke, Sienna, and Bailey were also still traveling on tour, which wouldn't end until just before Christmas. Jina and Cole were spending the holiday with her sister and brother-in-law in Madison. But the rest of the team was there, along with their spouses and kids, if they had them. Even Gabe Melrose had been included, although she noticed he stood awkwardly off to the side, his gaze constantly tracking Cassidy.

Rhy had refused to let Devon do much even though she'd recovered from being sick, and Joe, too, was protective of the very pregnant Elly, but everyone else pitched in.

Especially Flynn.

Many of the women were gathered in the living room, taking care of the babies. Several were pregnant, and those who weren't yet seemed to be interested in trying to be. Surprisingly, Taylor could relate, as she'd contacted the Department of Health and Human Services about Max Miller. He was with a foster family who wanted to adopt him. A pair of physicians who both worked at Children's Memorial Hospital.

As much as she wouldn't have minded taking Max in herself, she was reassured to know that Aaron and Maggie Monroe wanted to be Max's parents. And it sounded like Max would have a big brother too.

Taylor moved from the living room into the kitchen to help with meal prep. Much like Gabe, her gaze tracked Flynn. He had been wonderful over the past three weeks, supporting her writing to the point that she finished her book.

Her first book!

In truth, the romance had practically written itself, based in a large part on her own experience. Writing it down had proven to be cathartic.

She and Flynn had only stayed in the safe house for two days. The feds had moved quickly to arrest Allen and Irene Irving, finding them in the large house on Peabody Lake. Once they were no longer a threat, the federal agents had uncovered the entire money-laundering scheme. From what Brady and Doug had said, it sounded as if Allen was running an illegal gambling ring, funneling the cash through his companies and into the Brookland Bank. There were notes in Steve Miller's desk that indicated he'd stumbled across the money laundering that was being done practically under his nose and hadn't appreciated it. By tracking Steve's phone records, it appeared he had placed a call to Roman, who had met with him in Steve's home office. When he'd told Roman about his suspicions about his mother, Gail Lee, and her sister, Irene Irving, the plan to eliminate Steve and Robin had been put in motion.

What the Irvings hadn't counted on was Taylor being awake and caring for the baby. Understanding that she'd witnessed the murders and had been smart enough to evade being found by their hired gun, Nickoli Yurgis, had sent them into panic mode.

According to her cousin Jake, Nickoli had killed Roman out of anger when Roman had accused him of being an idiot for letting Taylor get away. Which in turn meant that Lyle and Jake had been tasked with finding Nickoli to finish him off as well. Since Nickoli's prints were found at her cousin's apartment, they assumed he'd tossed the place to find information on Taylor.

Detective Klem had survived the shooting and had agreed to cooperate with the investigation in exchange for being placed in protective custody. Flynn hadn't been happy with that but let it go when Cassidy pointed out how cops don't fare well in jail. Maybe Klem deserved to be placed in protective custody.

"Okay, everyone," Rhy called. "Dinner is ready."

As she, Flynn, Cassidy, Joe, and Rhy set platters of food on the table, the others gathered around the enormous dining room table. Everyone took a seat, except for Flynn, who stood next to Rhy.

"Before I say grace, I would like to ask Taylor to join me." Flynn's expression was so serious she worried he'd somehow learned bad news.

"Of course." She rose from her chair and went over to stand beside him. "We'll say grace together."

He smiled, then dropped to one knee. There was a collective gasp from the women in the room when he pulled out an engagement ring. "Taylor Rose, I love you very much. Will you please do me the honor of becoming my wife?"

"Yes, Flynn. A hundred times yes!" She threw herself into his arms, almost knocking him to the floor. He was strong enough to hold her close while rising to his feet.

"I love you," he whispered.

"I love you too," she whispered back.

The room erupted into applause, before Grayson said, "Hurry up already, it's time to eat!"

She and Flynn blushed, laughed, and kissed again before turning to face the room. They held hands and said grace, together.

And while Taylor had been upset to know her blood relatives had participated in brutal acts of murder, she realized in that moment that she had another family.

The tactical team family.

And having their love and support was all that mattered.

I HOPE you've enjoyed Flynn and Taylor's story! This Oath of Honor series has been a joy to write and of course there is still one more book to go to complete the series. Are you ready for Cassidy and Gabe's story in *Cassidy*? Click here!

DEAR READER

Thanks so much for reading my Oath of Honor series. I'm truly blessed to have wonderful readers like you. I hope you enjoyed Flynn and Taylor's story. I've been having so much fun bringing the Finnegans and even the Callahans back into these books. *Cassidy* is the final book in this series. I hope you'll take the time to read Cassidy and Gabe's Christmas story. It will be a great way to wrap up the series!

Don't forget, you can purchase eBooks or audiobooks directly from my website will receive a 15% discount by using the code **LauraScott15**.

I adore hearing from my readers! I can be found through my website at https://www.laurascottbooks.com, via Facebook at https://www.facebook.com/LauraScott Books, Instagram at https://www.instagram.com/laurascott books/, and Twitter https://twitter.com/laurascottbooks. Please take a moment to subscribe to my YouTube channel at youtube.com/@LauraScottBooks-wr1xl?sub_confirma- tion=1. Also take a moment to sign up for my monthly newsletter to learn about my new book releases! All subscribers receive a free novella not available for purchase on any platform.

Until next time,

Laura Scott

PS: Read on for a sneak peek of *Cassidy*.

CASSIDY

Chapter One

Snowflakes melted on his face. Blinking in confusion, he wondered why in the world he was outside lying on the cold, hard ground.

Pushing himself into a sitting position, he winced when his head throbbed with pain. He lifted his hand and found the source, a large bump and a gash of broken skin on the back of his head. When he saw the blood on his fingers, he grimaced and cleaned them with the freshly fallen snow.

He was in danger. The primitive instinct to get away couldn't be ignored. But as he gazed around, he didn't see a car or any other source of transportation.

Had he walked here? Or been dumped like garbage?

A sense of urgency hit hard. He needed to get far away before whoever had hit him returned. His thoughts were muddled; he couldn't remember what had happened. How he'd gotten here. Or why he was even there. Yet a single destination flashed in his mind.

Cassidy. He desperately needed to find Cassidy.

The image of a beautiful redhead was the only clear memory that came to the forefront of his mind. Somehow, he managed to get to his feet. His sneakered feet slipped in the snow, and he frowned when he realized his feet were wet and cold.

His hands too. He patted his coat pockets but didn't find gloves. Or a phone. He checked his back jeans pocket and shouldn't have been surprised to find his wallet was gone.

Had he been robbed?

Where exactly was he? Why was he here? And how long had he been unconscious?

Stepping carefully as he made his way down the slippery and deserted stretch of road, he scanned his surroundings. Something about the area was vaguely familiar. Not that he remembered ever having been there before, but because of the open space where some construction work appeared to have been done. Hadn't he overheard someone talking about a deserted building along an isolated stretch of road? The memory hung like mist in the air, just out of reach.

Why couldn't he remember?

The lights whizzing by made him realize he wasn't far from the interstate. Yet seeing the cars driving by wasn't exactly reassuring. What if the person who assaulted and robbed him returned?

A sense of panic hit hard. How would he manage to find Cassidy?

He stumbled but managed to stay upright. Nausea swirled in his belly, and the pain in his head grew worse with every step. Still, he kept moving, placing one foot in front of the other toward the highway that seemed impossibly far away.

As he grew closer, it was clear the road he was on crossed over the highway. A gas station sign gave him hope. He had to believe whoever was manning the gas station would allow him to borrow a phone.

Headlights from a car illuminated the road up ahead, and he instinctively ducked and darted into the clump of trees. His heart thundered in his chest as bitter fear coated his tongue. Were the bad guys coming back to finish him off?

Crouching down behind the bare trees, he watched as the vehicle rolled past. Maybe it was his imagination, but he thought the car moved slower than the weather conditions dictated.

A cautious driver? Maybe.

Yet once the car disappeared from his line of sight, he didn't move. Didn't head back out toward the gas station. He didn't trust anyone.

Except Cassidy.

But she wasn't there. He forced himself to stay where he was, despite the cold winter wind. When he began to shiver, he realized he was being foolish. There was no reason to risk hypothermia.

Leaving the relative shelter of the trees, he quickened his pace, lightly jogging to get the blood flowing through his veins. The motion made his head hurt, but he did his best to ignore the discomfort.

At this point, pain meant he was alive.

And he fully intended to stay that way.

He finally reached the gas station, thrilled beyond reason to see it included a small store. A bell jingled when he walked in, and he stood for a moment, savoring the warmth.

A dark-skinned man behind the counter eyed him suspiciously. He tried to smile, but his face felt frozen.

Maybe he had frostbite. He wasn't an expert on that sort of thing.

What was his expertise? Again, there was nothing but swirling mist where his memories should have been.

"May I help you?" The clerk's tone was clipped, as if he wasn't happy to have him as a customer.

He pulled his hands from his pockets, lifting them up in a gesture meant to reassure the clerk he meant no harm. "I'm sorry, but I've been robbed. I don't have my wallet or my phone. I was hoping I could borrow your phone to make a call."

"No phone," the clerk said. The way the guy's hand hovered under the desk out of sight made him worried he had a gun back there.

"Okay, look, I understand. You don't know me and don't trust me. But I can't walk all the way to . . ." He hesitated. Where did Cassidy live? Greenland? He didn't remember, but he did have a phone number in his head. At least, he hoped the number belonged to her. The way his brain was working, the number might belong to Mickey Mouse. "Would you please make a call for me? I need a friend to pick me up."

"Fine." The man scowled as if the simple task was a huge imposition. "What's the number?"

After a brief hesitation, he recited the digits. Why the number and Cassidy's face were the only clear images in his mind, he had no idea. But he was grateful the clerk had agreed to make the call.

He moved away from the door, grateful for the meager warmth. He eyed the snacks but wasn't hungry.

"No answer." The clerk waved his hand. "You go now."

He didn't move, trying to figure out what to do. Call the police? For some reason, he didn't want to go that route.

He and the clerk jumped when the phone rang. With reluctance, the clerk answered. "Hello? Yes, just one moment." The clerk scowled as he slid the phone under the glass window separating them.

He grabbed the phone and lifted it to his ear. "Cassidy? Is that you?"

"Who is this?" a familiar female voice asked.

"I, uh . . ." He frowned, wondering why his name didn't pop into his mind. "I need a ride. I've been robbed and need a ride."

"Gabe? Is that you? You've really been robbed?"

"Yes. I don't have my phone or my wallet." A sense of calm washed over him. The name Gabe sounded right. Although it seemed strange not to know his own name. "I'm sorry, but I need a ride."

"Okay, where are you calling from?"

"From a gas station. Um, what's the address?" he asked the clerk. When he rattled it off, Gabe repeated it for Cassidy.

"I know that area, I'll be there as quickly as possible. Are you sure you're okay?"

No, he wasn't okay. But of course, he answered, "Yes. I'll be fine. Just get here soon."

"I'm on my way." Cassidy disconnected from the call.

Dazed and relieved, he slid the device under the glass. "Thank you. My friend Cassidy will be here soon."

The clerk nodded, his expression indicating Gabe was welcome to stay inside to wait.

He lifted his hand to the back of his head again. What had happened? A simple robbery?

Or something more sinister?

For some strange reason, he felt certain there was nothing simple about what had happened to him.

Danger lurked nearby. Too bad he couldn't remember anything about who might have come after him or why.

TACTICAL POLICE OFFICER Cassidy Sommer quickly dressed and headed out to the garage attached to her condo. Why on earth was Gabe way out near the Wildflower Motel? Had he met someone there and been robbed?

She didn't want to believe the team's tech guru would do something illegal, but she was at a loss as to why he was so far away, considering he lived closer to the lakefront in White Gull Bay. Upon reaching the interstate, she hit the gas, speeding as fast as she dared. The hour wasn't that late, only ten thirty at night, which meant traffic wasn't a problem. Hopefully, she wouldn't be pulled over by the state patrol.

It was difficult to imagine a legitimate reason for Gabe to be so far outside the city. She considered Gabe to be a good friend; she felt certain she'd have known if he'd done something illegal. Besides, Gabe worked for the Milwaukee Police Department. As a civilian, yes, but he still needed to keep his record clean.

Soft snowflakes melted when they hit her windshield, and the outside temperature hovered at thirty-two degrees. Christmas, her favorite holiday, was only three weeks away, and she was planning a party for the entire tactical team for the weekend before the actual holiday since she knew her teammates would want to spend that time with their families. Joe Kingsley and Elly in particular were expecting their first baby on the day after Christmas.

All her teammates were getting married or engaged. She was still the odd one out but tried not to focus on that. She had been engaged once, but the guy who'd claimed to love her abruptly decided he didn't want to be married to a cop. Last she'd heard, Wade Morris was happily married to an accountant.

Goody for him, she thought with a sigh. Obviously, he hadn't loved her as much as she had cared for him.

Reminding herself she was better off without Wade, she spied the exit for the Wildflower Motel. The gas station was located about a mile to the north, so she turned right after getting off the interstate.

She pulled into the parking lot of the gas station, wondering how Gabe had gotten there. There was no sign of his car, a tomato-red SUV. She hadn't seen it in the motel parking lot either.

Had he taken a rideshare out here? Was that the person who'd robbed him?

She killed the engine and slid out from behind the wheel. Ducking her chin into her coat collar, she hurried inside the building. It reeked of tobacco, either from the stock of cigarettes or because the clerk smoked while on duty.

"Cassidy!" Gabe's expression brightened when he saw her. "Thanks for coming."

"What on earth happened?" Gabe's brown hair and the side of his face was matted and smeared with blood. Her heart squeezed as she realized he'd been assaulted. "Who did this to you?"

"I don't know." A flicker of uncertainty darkened his brown eyes. It took her a minute to realize he wasn't wearing his glasses. He'd recently gotten contacts but mentioned how he hadn't liked wearing them at work. "Can we please get out of here?"

"Yes, of course." She glanced at the clerk who was watching them suspiciously. She smiled and nodded at him. "Thank you for allowing my friend to borrow your phone."

The clerk shrugged. "It is fine. Just please go now."

"Yes, thanks," Gabe added.

She took his arm and steered him toward the door. But rather than going outside, Gabe stopped, peering through the glass into the night. She frowned, wondering what was wrong with him, but then he moved forward to open the door.

"We need to hurry," he said as they stepped outside. "I don't like being out in the open like this."

What? She glanced at Gabe, wondering what on earth he was talking about. This wasn't the Gabe she knew. He was acting as if he was a cop who needed to track down a perp.

Not the tech team expert who supported her and her fellow officers while they were on scene facing danger.

"You're worrying me," she said as they crossed to her black SUV. "Where's your car? Was that stolen too?"

"My car?" Gabe turned in his seat, looking confused. "I don't know. What kind of car do I drive?"

Again, she felt as if she'd been dropped into an alternate universe. "You're asking me what kind of car you drive?" She frowned, searching his gaze "You know what car you drive. You were so happy to have the only bright-red SUV in the parking lot of our precinct."

"Precinct?" Gabe clipped his seatbelt in place. "We're cops?"

"I'm a cop. You're our tech analyst." As she put the SUV into gear and pulled out of the parking lot, she didn't try to hide her frustration. "What is going on with you, Gabe? Why are you acting like this?"

He didn't answer for a long moment. "I guess I should tell you everything."

"Yes, you should." Cass braced herself. "What have you gotten involved in?"

"I don't know." Gabe lifted a hand to his head, winced, then lowered it again. "I don't know anything. I didn't remember my name until you mentioned it on the phone. I don't know why I was hit on the head and knocked unconscious. I don't know why I woke up way out in the middle of nowhere without my wallet, phone, or any cash. I don't remember anything."

Seriously? She glanced at him, trying to understand.

"I wish I could tell you what is going on, but I can't. I don't remember anyone being with me or striking out at me." He turned to meet her gaze, and the troubled expression on his face tugged at her heartstrings. "I only remember you, Cassidy."

She blew out a breath, reeling from what he was saying. Part of her wanted to scoff at the idea that he had amnesia. That Gabe Melrose couldn't remember his name or his impressive career within the tactical team.

But the man she knew wasn't this good of an actor. Gabe might be big into gaming and was unreasonably excited over technological advances, but he didn't pretend to be something he wasn't. He was up front and honest about his strengths and weaknesses.

A trait she'd found endearing.

She forced herself to think like a cop. Gabe had been assaulted and robbed. And as such, he was the victim of a crime. "Okay, you have a head injury and can't remember anything. I'll take you straight to Trinity Medical Center to be medically evaluated."

"No! We can't go to the hospital." He grabbed her arm. "Please, Cassidy, just take me home. I'm sure I'll remember everything by morning."

"Gabe, you're bleeding and have a head injury. Of course, you need to be checked out. The gash on your head likely needs stitches."

"No, please. I don't want to go." His voice sounded panicked. "Not yet."

She glanced at him with concern. "What is really going on here, Gabe?"

"I don't know." He closed his eyes for a moment, then turned to look at her. "I wish I did understand why I'm in this situation. All I can say is that my gut is telling me to lie low. To keep off the grid. To make it difficult to find me."

"Who? To make it difficult for who to find you?" She didn't want to risk his head injury getting worse. But the way he was so emphatic about not going in to be seen was weighing on her. What if he was right? What if someone was still out there, waiting for the chance to finish him off?

"I don't know!" His voice was tortured. "If I knew, I'd tell you so you could help me find and arrest him!"

"Him? You remember the assailant was a man?" she asked.

He sighed heavily. "No, I don't remember. I guess it could be a woman who clocked me in the back of the head, but I assumed the person responsible was a man. Someone with the strength to toss me out of the car and onto the side of the road."

Cassidy didn't point out that she, Raelyn, and Jina—the only female members of the tactical team—were capable of that and more. Because he was probably right. It wasn't likely the assailant was a woman, but one thing she'd learned over the course of her career was to not make any assumptions.

She and several of her teammates had trusted the wrong person before. Anything was possible.

But that didn't help in making the right decision about whether to take him to the hospital or to give in to his request to be taken home.

"We could try to reach out to Alanna," she finally said. "I'm sure she has the ability to stitch up a wound."

"No. I can't allow you to drag anyone else into this." Gabe curled his fingers into fists, another gesture she'd never noticed from him before. He seemed very different from the Gabe she'd worked with for four years now.

"I would rather—" she began, but he cut her off.

"No. I'm begging you to take me home. If my memory is still foggy by the morning, I'll agree to be checked out." He met her gaze. "I promise."

"Fine." She threw up her hand. "Have it your way. I don't ever remember you being this stubborn before, Gabe. It's not the least bit logical not to have a doctor examine a head injury."

"I'm sorry." His tone was subdued, as if she'd wounded him by speaking her thoughts. "I can't explain it other than to say I have this weird sense that I'm in danger. That I need to remember what happened before I do anything else."

She gave in, mostly because she knew how important it was to trust her instincts. If Gabe felt as if he was in danger, then she needed to take his feelings into consideration.

"Maybe we shouldn't go to your place," she said, breaking the silence. "You can stay with me."

He hesitated. "I don't want to put you out. The thought

of going home doesn't scare me the way going to the hospital does."

That didn't make any sense. Yet rather than continuing to argue, she passed the exit that would take them to her condo and kept going toward White Gull Bay.

She'd give in to a certain extent. If he wanted to go home, she'd stay with him at his place. She knew Gabe had inherited the house from his father, who had passed away two years ago. Not only did he have a nice guest bedroom, but he was in no condition to toss her out.

For one thing, Gabe was tall and skinny, despite the way he devoured snacks like he feared a worldwide shortage loomed on the horizon. But even more so because she and Raelyn had begun working out with Jina at her MMA gym. She didn't have Jina's skill or strength yet, but she was learning.

She could be stubborn too.

"What's my last name?" Gabe's question came from left field. "If you don't mind me asking."

"Melrose. Your name is Gabriel Thomas Melrose. Your dad's name was Thomas." She glanced at him. "He died two years ago."

He frowned. "I wish I could remember him."

She had no idea what to say to that. Gabe and his father had been very close, but that wasn't the case with his mother who had remarried ten years ago. She'd traded up, as Gabe had put it, giving up his father the police detective for a wealthy lawyer.

Gabe's home was a small ranch, two houses in from the corner. She pulled into the driveway, frowning when she didn't see any Christmas decorations. Gabe had mentioned his plan to put up a tree this year, but it appeared he hadn't followed through.

She parked in the driveway and slid out from behind the wheel. Gabe headed to the garage and entered a code on the keypad. Which was probably a good thing, since he'd been robbed and didn't have his keys.

When the garage door opened, though, she saw his red SUV parked inside. What in the world? Gabe had clearly left the car behind on purpose.

He looked just as surprised to see the SUV. He glanced at her. "This is my car?"

"Yes." Alarm bells rang in the back of her mind, and she reached for her gun. "Stay back. I'm going in first."

He scowled, looking as if he wanted to argue, but stepped to the side to give her room to squeeze past the car. The door leading from the garage to the house didn't look tampered with, but she didn't lower her weapon. Twisting the handle, she pushed the door open but hung back to wait and listen.

Hearing nothing, she stepped across the threshold, sweeping her gun over the area as she went. It was dark inside, but lights from the neighbors' Christmas decorations along with the streetlight outside provided enough illumination for her to see.

The interior of the house stopped her cold. The place had been trashed. Her gaze went from the shattered oversized TV screen to the sofa cushions that were cut open and strewn around the room to the kitchen drawers that had been opened and dumped onto the floor.

This was no robbery. Whoever had done this had been searching for something. She only wished she knew exactly what they'd wanted.